STAND YOUR GROUND
AMERICAN STRONG SERIES – BOOK 1

BY CHRIS PIKE

Stand Your Ground
Book 1
American Strong Series
by Chris Pike
Copyright © 2018. All Rights Reserved

Without limiting the rights under copyright reserved above, no part of this publication may be reproduced, stored, or introduced into a retrieval system, or transmitted in any form, or by any means (electronically, mechanical, photocopying, recording or otherwise) without the proper written permission of the copyright owner, except in the case of brief quotations embodied in critical articles and reviews.

This book is a work of fiction. People, places, events, and situations are the product of the author's imagination, except in the case of authenticity. Any resemblance to actual persons, living or dead, or historical events, is purely coincidental.

To my readers: Thank you. This story would not have been possible without you and your encouragement. Y'all are the best! And to my family who has put up with all my crazy ideas and work-shopping sessions, y'all are the best too.
—Chris

"You were given this life because you are strong enough to live it."
—Unknown

"When you have exhausted all possibilities, remember this: You haven't."
—Thomas Edison

I've tried so hard to forget. I buried those memories long ago, deep in my mind, covered by the weight of despair. I tossed them in the ocean and watched them sink slowly in the murky water, covered by the pressure of ten thousand fathoms. Now I must resurrect them.
Why?
So the next generation will know.
So they will survive.

Ella Strong, survivor

CHAPTER 1

Houston, Texas
Current Day

It was exactly 7:10 in the morning on a late April day. I remembered it clearly because it was the last normal day of my life.

A spectacular sunrise greeted me as I drove along the freeway to my high school, weaving in and out of lanes trying to get to class on time. I didn't attend the local school; rather the one for the performing arts located several miles down the freeway from my house.

I paid no attention to the chattering of the DJs on the radio. Instead, my gaze gravitated to low-hanging clouds on the horizon where the orange glow of the morning sun illuminated the odd shapes.

If I hadn't known any better, I would have sworn the clouds were newly forming mountaintops or hills, bubbling up like hot magma, peeking over the massive Houston freeway exchange of the 610 Loop and Interstate 10. The clouds were growing increasingly dark and heavy by the second, and I hoped I could beat them before I arrived at school.

If only they had been rain clouds, life would have been so easy. But they weren't, and I didn't beat them, nor did anybody else.

* * *

STAND YOUR GROUND

The day had started out the same as all the rest. Get up, shower, eat a quick breakfast. Beat the clock.

With a towel wrapped around my damp hair, I walked into the kitchen to check breakfast options. Classes were winding down and I couldn't wait until I graduated so I could begin the next chapter of my life.

A fresh pot of coffee had been brewed, the aroma teasing my taste buds. I poured a cup and splashed some sugar and cream in it. I tasted it, deciding it needed a bit more cream. I had gotten hooked on coffee during the fall semester when I had to study for tests late at night after basketball practice. Now I couldn't function without it.

The morning news drummed in the background on our high definition big screen TV while my dad ate breakfast at the table.

"Morning, Dad," I said, still half asleep, taking a sip of coffee. I removed the towel and ran my fingers through my hair to untangle it, patting it dry with the towel.

"Morning, Ellie Bellie."

"Please don't call me that. It makes me feel bad." My shoulders shrank down and my good mood vanished. As a child, people referred to me as a 'big girl' and the label adversely affected me. I thought something was wrong with me, and it bothered me for a long time. Several years ago I had a late growth spurt, and during that summer my baby fat turned into womanly curves. All the boys started to notice, all except for the one I thought mattered.

I didn't consider myself fat or big, but I suppose at 5'10" I could be intimidating to some people.

"Ella, I'm sorry," my dad mumbled as he scarfed down another spoonful of cereal. "I forgot how cruel the kids had been to you."

"Elementary school was bad when I was the new kid on the block, then being taller than all the boys until recently was really bad. But, hey, I've got a basketball scholarship for the next four years, so I got the last laugh."

"I'll say. And remember, you're my strong girl." He winked.

I laughed and rolled my eyes. "Dad, you're so funny. Of course I'm a strong girl. Our last name is Strong after all."

"Well, you're still a strong girl. You have a natural athletic ability which will get you through whatever life throws at you. And you're competitive. I've seen you on the court, running faster and jumping higher than your competition. You put a lot of points on the board, Ella. Regardless of how the game is played, winning does matter. Don't forget, you nearly singlehandedly propelled your high school girls' basketball team to the playoffs."

"I've done a lot of practicing."

"Ella, don't downplay what you've done. I've tried to prepare you to be a leader in whatever you do. You're showing signs it's paying off, and being a captain of your basketball team was the first test of your leadership qualities."

"Dad, you're embarrassing me."

"Sorry," my dad said. "Listen, I was thinking we should celebrate before you leave for basketball camp. When does that start?"

"Mid-June, so I only have a couple of months until I'm gone."

"Then let's not waste any more time. I have a question for you, Ella. Doesn't your college have a competitive rifle team?"

"It does."

"Let's go to the shooting range to get you some more practice. You're a natural with a gun, and joining the team would be a good way to meet some boys."

"We'll see about that."

"Ella, I know you've had a special relationship with Tommy for many years, but he doesn't treat you like a girlfriend."

"Dad, let's not talk about that. Not now. Tell you what. Let's go to the shooting range this weekend."

"Deal."

"Dad, I'll miss being here."

"Don't be sad," he said. "You'll make new friends."

Our morning banter was interrupted by the loud jingle of a breaking news story on the big screen TV. My attention was square on the action. Reporters and cameramen were jostling for position on the tarmac at one of the airports.

"Is that at Intercontinental Airport?" I asked.

"I don't think so. It's probably Ellington Field, the one in southwest Houston. It's the airfield presidents normally fly in and out of when they make a trip here."

I gave my dad a puzzled look. "Why?"

"For security reasons."

"Oh, right."

A camera zoomed to a horde of men wearing serious expressions, dark sunglasses, dark suits, and guns drawn. They'd taken a shooter's stance, crouched with their legs hip wide apart, both hands on their guns. Another group of the same kind of men held back the reporters, clamoring for a

STAND YOUR GROUND

better position.

"What's going on?" I sat down on the sofa near the TV to get a better look. "Are those Secret Service?"

"I believe so."

"Did you see that, Dad? One of them is putting on a gas mask. Are they being gassed?"

"I doubt it. Probably only a precaution."

"He's running away. I thought they were supposed to protect the president with their lives?"

"They should protect the president at all costs. Perhaps he's been called away. Air Force One is in the background," my dad said, pointing at the TV. "The American flag is on the tail, and *United States of America* is written on the side. The president was in town to give a fundraising speech at one of the colleges, but the news indicated it was cancelled."

"Why?"

"Must be something important going on in the Middle East, especially since we bombed Syria." My dad shook his head. "Who would gas their own people? Did you see the pictures of those poor people, including women and children? I can't imagine the suffering. Now there's been all sorts of chatter about Russia showing the world who's boss."

"What'dya mean?"

"It's the hypersonic weapon the Russians have been testing. I read about it in the news."

"The what?"

"A hypersonic weapon. In a nutshell, it's attached to an intercontinental ballistic missile, and has the capability to sit on top of the atmosphere by using aerodynamic forces. Good for them, bad for us, because the United States doesn't have any weapons to defend against it for various reasons."

"Such as?"

"For one, it can travel five times the speed of sound. Plus, it can turn on a dime, making it difficult to track. We have gaps in our missile defense system. I've read the weapon can defeat any of the most advanced missile defense systems, including ours."

"Why hasn't our country developed its own hypersonic weapon? It couldn't have been a secret if it was in the news."

"Budget cuts probably. National debt, politics. The reasons go on and on."

"Do you think the Russians are about to attack us with that weapon? If so, I guess I shouldn't go to school."

CHRIS PIKE

My dad laughed. "Ella, go on to school. I seriously doubt the Russians would hit Houston first. They'd go after Washington, D.C."

"Maybe not," I countered. "I may only be eighteen, but I understand the significance of the president's speech being cancelled, and all the activity around Air Force One at Ellington field." My dad responded with silence. "Where exactly is the president?"

"I guess he's en route to Ellington Field from the college where he was supposed to speak. I'm sure he's being whisked back to D.C. for some important cabinet meeting, or whatever nonsensical meetings happen in D.C."

"Do you think Russia will bomb us?"

"Ella," my dad said, using his best comforting voice, the kind he used when I scraped my knee as a kid then went running to him crying for a band-aid. "Don't worry about Houston. Washington, D.C. or New York City would get it before anybody else, like on nine-eleven." He put down his spoon. "What you do need to worry about are your grades. You still need to keep your grades up, even though you graduate in a month."

"It's all good. I got an A on my last science test."

"Great! Your mom and I are both proud of you."

"Thanks, Dad. Enough talk about the end of the world. I'll get ready for school."

"Good choice."

I opened the freezer door to peruse the selection of frozen waffles. My choices were blueberry, chocolate, and something masquerading as strawberry. They all tasted like cardboard, but with enough real butter and syrup, anything was palatable.

"Where's Mom?" I asked.

"Still in bed. She's not feeling well at all."

I wanted to burst out crying or scream at the world at how unfair her illness was, being beyond my mother's control, or the doctor's, or my dad's.

"What did the last lab report indicate?" I asked. I placed two frozen waffles in the toaster, pushed the button down to toast them, then poured myself a glass of milk.

He lowered his reading glasses and peered at me over the top of the rims. He shook his head. "Not good."

I swallowed a lump in my throat. "I can stay home with her if you need me to."

"Ella, you need to go to school. Besides, your mom doesn't want you to

STAND YOUR GROUND

see her suffer, or for you to miss any classes. She has her cell phone right next to her, so if she needs me, she can call me." He took his cereal bowl to the sink and ran water in it. "By the way, you'll need to take your sister to school."

"I don't have time," I protested. "You take her. If we went to the same high school, it would be no big deal, but it's the opposite direction I need to go."

"Please, Ella. Don't start. Why do you and your sister fight so much? When I was your age, Uncle Grant and I—"

"Were the best of friends." I rolled my eyes. "I've heard it a thousand times. You and Uncle Grant were the worst of enemies when you were kids, then when you were teens, you became the best of friends. May and I are only the former."

"Grant and I *are*, and continue to be best friends, Ella. When you get older, when things are tough, when your mom and I are dead and buried, when your friends have their own lives, maybe your husband has left you for another—"

"Dad! I'm not even married and now you're telling me my husband will run away with another woman?"

"When any or all of that happens, you'll understand your sister will be the only person you can count on."

I huffed. "I doubt it."

"Perhaps, but your mother and I have helped out Grant quite a bit these last few years. I'm sure you would do the same for May, and vice versa."

"Dad, where is Uncle Grant? Is he still at the ranch, taking care of things?"

"He is." My dad wiped the kitchen counter with a sponge. "It's better for all of us if the old ranch house stays occupied. When a house stays vacant too long, it falls into disrepair. Besides, when Grant fell on hard times from his business failing, then his wife leaving him, I couldn't abandon him. I'm not sure he recovered from his wife leaving him and taking their son with her. Family needs to help one another out if they can. When your mother and I are gone, when you've grown apart from your high school friends, you'll have your sister. We raised you to be friends."

"Right," I said sarcastically. "Look how that turned out." I walked over to the pantry, hoping we still had syrup. I picked up the plastic bottle and glanced in dismay at the pathetic amount of syrup. Someone had put it back in with only a half teaspoon of syrup left. I tossed it in the garbage can where it landed with a thunk.

My dad squeezed the sponge and set it down. "I hope that changes. So, Ella, will you do me a favor and take May to school? I've got an important meeting at eight this morning at the lab and I can't be late."

"Okay." I let out an audible sigh of defeat. "She won't like it. She doesn't even like being in the same room with me."

My dad snorted. "Don't I know it!"

"I gotta hurry up now before I'm late to school." The toaster dinged and popped up the waffles. I spread a thin layer of peanut butter on them and topped it with a swirl of honey. I ate them as fast as I could and gulped down the last of the coffee.

"Thanks, Ella. I appreciate it."

CHAPTER 2

I was the older of two daughters in a normal family. My mother fawned over my sister, younger by two years, who got lucky in the gene pool. I admit she was a beauty, with sparkling sea-green eyes, blonde hair, and a perfect petite figure. She was a cheerleader too, and she could do the most amazing flips. She was an anomaly among her tall, big-boned family members.

I always thought my sister's beauty and athletic prowess made her the lucky one. Actually, I was the lucky one in the gene pool, or unlucky, depending on one's perspective.

Why did I waste those formative years being jealous over my sister? I was mean to her in subtle ways–a disapproving look or a catty comment. I pushed her out of my life because of what? Sibling rivalry? Jealousy? The arguments we had were so trivial.

"Come on, May, we have to go *now*!" I screamed at her as I slammed the front door shut. In a fit of pique I stormed out to the car and backed it out of the driveway, impatiently tapping my fingers on the steering wheel. She darted out of the house and hopped into the car.

"What's the matter, forgot your lip gloss?" I said snidely.

"Shut up. You could use some lip gloss."

We drove the rest of the way in silence, each of us fuming at whatever perceived grievance we had. With us both sulking, the ten minute drive

STAND YOUR GROUND

seemed to take forever. I stopped the car in front of the school because I wasn't about to placate her by driving all the way to the back and out of my way. She could walk the few extra steps. I didn't care if her perfect hair got messed up by the humidity.

"Don't let the door hit your big butt on the way out," I said with a wicked smile. "Hurry up and hit the road before you make me late."

She glared at me.

Time has muddled all the hurt I felt towards my sister. We were close when we were children. We did all the usual things little girls do like putting makeup on one another, playing dress-up, playing with dolls, riding bikes. Those were the memories I want to cherish. Those were the ones that kept me going when times got tough. Later, in our teenage years, we drifted apart. I was the studious one, always curious why things worked, and if they didn't, then I worked tirelessly to repair them. Often when I asked my dad what I should do, he told me to figure it out myself. I spent a lot of time with my dad, an engineer and biochemist who introduced me to the wonders of science.

In a normal time, I would like to have gone to college and majored in chemistry or one of the sciences. I would have lived in a dorm, gone to classes, had years to transition from my teenage years to adulthood.

Instead, I had a zero to sixty experience in a different type of schooling, and I liked to think I graduated with a PhD in survival.

As I drove closer to my school, those clouds on the horizon exploded into a huge billowing mass, darkening the sky. They were roiling now, like dirty boiling water. Probably some storm clouds moving in from the Gulf of Mexico. I shrugged it off, thinking it happened all the time. I didn't pay too much attention to them because my thoughts were about the cutest boy in school. My breathing increased and my hands became clammy thinking about him. I'd had a crush on Tommy ever since he saved me from a bully in third grade.

I wanted him so much it hurt, and it bordered on the obsessive, thinking about him first thing in the morning, and he was the last thing on my mind at night. I had to have him. I had to prove to everybody I could get him and I would do anything to do so. I was stubborn, because when I set my mind on a goal, I achieved it. I guess my dad was right–I am competitive.

I parked my car in a strategic spot in the school parking lot, and sat for a minute listening to the radio. I pretended to be texting on my cell phone, waiting for Tommy. As my languid thumbs nervously worked the keypad, he whipped his car in the spot next to mine. Dust and gravel flew up in the air. Nonchalantly, I waved at him. He had a splash of red hair, and freckles all over his face. He flashed a smile, and I knew he smiled only for me.

"Hey, Ella. What's going on?" he asked with a confident upwards motion of his head.

We both got out of our cars.

"Hi, Tommy," I mewed. My gaze naturally fell to my feet, and an expression of fright appeared on my face. I hadn't trimmed my toenails. The polish was chipped. Surely, he'd notice.

My hair.

It was a tangled mess.

Oh crap.

Surreptitiously, I ran my fingers through my hair to smooth it, then touched my dry, cracked lips.

I should've put lip gloss on.

"Did you do the homework for Mrs. Latham's class?" Tommy asked, impatiently tapping his foot on the gravel lot.

"Yes," I said coyly, twirling a lock of my long, thick brunette hair with my index finger. I batted my eyelashes at him. I'd seen that in the movies and it always worked.

"Give it to me."

I stopped twirling my hair. I guess the movies weren't right after all. I fumbled around in my backpack then handed the homework to Tommy.

His hand brushed against my arm when he snatched the homework away from me. Did he long for me in the way I longed for him? I waited for his eyes to meet mine, but they never did. Perhaps he'd walk me to class, and I imagined him putting his arms around me, bringing me close.

I would have done anything for him. All he had to do was ask.

Tommy was tall and athletic, and captain of the baseball team. His muscles rippled under his uniform when he took a swing at a ball, and a collective sigh came from the stands. All the girls pined for him. I could tell by the way they looked at him, giggling and whispering when he walked by. It made me jealous because we had a deal.

Tommy was dyslexic. He got numbers and letters all mixed up in his head. But he was smart. He could recount, word for word, the Constitution of the United States and the first Ten Amendments. I could barely get through the preamble. In exchange for me helping him with his homework, he'd take me to dances and movies.

We'd sit together in class, and during tests I would give him the answers by using a secret code. A wiggle here, or a tap of the foot might

STAND YOUR GROUND

mean answer C for question two. Sometimes I scratched my head, or twirled my hair. Left hand meant odd numbered pages, right hand even numbered. People thought I was twitchy, but it wasn't the case. One time someone asked me if I had Tourettes. I told them I had a mild case and it spread like wildfire throughout the school.

"Thanks, Ella. I appreciate it. You even forged my name. It's exactly like mine," Tommy said, inspecting the paper. "You sure all the math problems are correct?"

"I think so."

"They better be. Graduation is right around the corner, and the scholarship I applied for depends on it."

"I promise I did them all correctly." I hated that I was being reduced to a blubbering schoolgirl.

"Okay," he said.

"I can tutor you this Saturday," I said hopefully.

"Can't. I'm going out with friends."

I didn't even respond.

"See you later." He trotted off to class leaving me behind.

I sighed and slumped my shoulders. Right when I thought he didn't care, he turned back around to wink at me, and a wide, crinkly smile crept over my face. The cutest boy in class winked at me, and I felt like the prettiest girl in the world.

My school was located a few blocks from the freeway. Even the concrete sound barrier didn't prevent us from hearing the roar of the cars in the classroom, especially the big eighteen wheelers. Those were the noisiest. They made the windows shake too. I had started to walk across the gravel parking lot when the crashes on the freeway occurred, one after another, metal crunching against metal, making unnatural sounds.

In the distance, the soft wailing of ambulances sliced through the humid morning air, and I noticed an odd smell. The cloud from the Gulf was enormous, and in the middle of it was a strange green bubbling mass.

Must be from pollution, I thought.

We were close to the oil refineries near the coast, and when the wind blew right, I could smell the toxic odor of chemicals.

I shivered in the morning dampness.

All sorts of thoughts went through my head. Perhaps there had been an oil refinery fire, or a ship had blown up in the channel, resulting in smoke blowing inland.

It started to rain a bit. Perhaps a late season tropical storm had blown in from the Gulf, and the rain had caused the roads to become slick. I didn't remember my dad talking about the weather the night before. Every evening he stayed glued to the six o'clock news and the weather. He hailed from a ranching family where weather was all important. It was more important than the farm animals, or the death of a family member. Too much rain and the crops would be destroyed; too little and they would dry up and wither away into dry, crunchy nothingness.

Amazingly, my dad still owned the family ranch. When he didn't work overtime at the lab, we went to the ranch on weekends. It was a beautiful place, nestled in the fertile Hill Country of Central Texas. A branch lined with pecan trees ran through our land, and pools of spring fed water teemed with perch and bullfrogs. Many times we ate a meal of fried perch my dad and I caught in one of those pools.

I watched squirrels jumping from tree to tree, a canopy so thick the squirrels never had to set foot on the ground. Good crops could still be grown too. My mother canned fruits and vegetables from the garden, and stacked them in the cellar where it was cool for later use. The cellar was damp and dark, and full of spindly, harmless daddy longleg spiders.

Some days at the ranch my dad would take me hunting. May couldn't be bothered, which was fine by me because I had my dad all to myself, and we bonded on those cherished walks through the woods. He showed me the edible plants, and which ones had medicinal purposes, pointed out the best places to hunt, how to track game, and taught me how to handle a firearm.

When I was little, my dad built a treehouse at the ranch, deep in the woods. He positioned it high in a century-old oak tree near the creek bottom. He said it was my special hiding place, and we never told anyone about it. The thick dark green foliage hid it from prying eyes, especially on the ground, but if I stood on my toes in the treehouse, I had a marvelous view of the surrounding valley and woods where the cedar trees created a natural windbreak. The area teemed with deer, turkeys, wild hogs, doves, and quail.

In the orchard, planted long ago, pecan trees were heavy with nuts, and the peach trees bore delicious fruit which ripened in the early summer. Wild mustang grapes grew on fence posts, and in the pasture, patches of two foot tall wheat still grew.

When I was little I would run through the golden wheat, amber grains blowing in the wind like an incoming wave on the beach. I skipped through the grain, my hands threading through the florets, catching seeds.

STAND YOUR GROUND

I'd glance over my shoulders, pretending to be chased by a wild animal. I'd run faster as the imaginary beast closed in on my heels, snapping at me. Right as it was about to catch me, I'd find a tree and scramble up the branches until I was high in the tree, safe.

A gust of wind blew in over the parking lot, and it whooshed all around me. I leaned into it to keep from blowing over. Some sort of fine particles in the wind and rain assaulted me as I hurried towards my classroom. My nose twitched and I sneezed.

What was that smell?

I couldn't place it; neither would I ever forget it.

The wind pushing me along, I ran to my classroom. My first class of the day was theatre with Mr. Kimble. He was a grumpy old man who had been teaching too long. The plays didn't excite him any longer, and it showed in his mood. He always yelled at us to be quiet or to sit down. We didn't pay much attention to him.

I raced alongside the brick building to the outside door of the theatre room, but I was late. The bell rang and the loud clanging noise, like cymbals smashing together, hurt my ears. The wind blew harder and I struggled to open the heavy metal door. Suddenly the vacuum broke and the door flew open. The wind caught it and slammed it against the outer wall, making a huge ruckus.

I stood in the doorway, the wind and rain washing over me. My classmates turned in unison to stare at me. The wind rushed into the room, rustling loose papers off the desks and scattering them. My classmates chased after the papers. I waited for Mr. Kimble to start his tirade. He turned in my direction and his eyebrows furrowed in his annoying way. His lips pursed to hiss my name but before he could utter a sound, confusion overtook him. He clutched his chest and fell to the floor in a silent heap.

He was surely acting, trying to be dramatic. It was a pathetic attempt.

"Cindrella! What have you done?" Tommy yelled, using my full name. He must be mad at me. A breath caught in my throat. Only my mother and father call me by my real name when they are mad at me. My mother insisted on naming me after the fairytale princess, though with a slightly different spelling, and my sister after the cosmetic giant, Maybelline. She must have hoped for a fairytale life for us.

"I didn't do anything. He's acting," I protested.

"Get in here and close the door." He huffed and crossed his arms.

"Lauren, call the front desk. Mr. Kimble must be sick!" I shouted to my best friend. I stepped into the room and tossed my backpack on a desk.

"There's no answer!" she screamed from across the room.

"Try again!" I shouted. "Haley, check if Mr. Kimble is okay."

My classmate bent down to check for a pulse. "He's not breathing!" she shrieked. "What should I do?"

"Start CPR."

"What! And put my mouth on his? That would be like kissing him."

"Then get somebody else to do it."

In the back of the class someone screamed. It was a real scream, not the fake kind we learned for theatrical plays. Another classmate fainted, then another, and another.

"I'll go get Mrs. Watkins," I announced. "She's been trained in first aid."

I rushed past the students hovering around Mr. Kimble, racing toward the inside door leading to the hallway. I pushed open the door to find the hallway in absolute chaos. Mrs. Watkins lay sprawled on the floor in an unnatural position with her eyes wide open and her mouth frozen in a horrified grimace. A sea of students ran past her, coughing and gasping for air. Some had fallen, curled into balls on the floor, moaning.

"Mrs. Watkins, are you okay?" I yelled. There was no response. "Mrs. Watkins?" I cried faintly through a strained voice. Her unfocused eyes were glassy, and her skin had taken on the color of old chalk. Then it occurred to me. *Oh God, she's dead!* My heart beat so hard I could feel the thumping in my ears. I had never seen a dead person before, and a deep welling of revulsion rose in me. I clutched my stomach and bent over, my hand instinctively going to my mouth. I gagged and almost threw up.

"Help!" I coughed out. No one paid any attention to me.

I ran to my theatre class, where the scene inside was just as ghastly. My classmates had fallen on the floor, one on top of another, and a few were gasping for air. Chairs had been knocked over, and papers were strewn around the room. Tommy stood on the stage. His mouth hung open, ready to scream words that wouldn't form.

"Tommy, what's happening?" I screamed. There was no answer. He stood there, not moving. "What's wrong with you? Do something!"

He didn't move. He stood frozen, his arms at his sides, staring at the lifeless bodies on the floor. I ran over to him, put my hands on his shoulders, and shook him. "Tommy!"

"I...I don't know," he stammered. "Something is wrong. Let's get outta

STAND YOUR GROUND

here." He scowled at me and jerked my arm. "Come on, let's go!"

"We can't. We need to call for help."

"You can stay if you want to, but I'm leaving."

"Wait," I pleaded. "Don't leave me here by myself." It was no use. He ran out, leaving me behind in the classroom.

There were no more sounds or gurgling noises of people dying, only the silence of escaping souls.

My heart raced and my hands became clammy. Each tick of the clock on the wall was magnified, and my ears thumped with each movement of the second hand. Terrified, I covered my ears with both hands and ran outside.

In the unreal morning darkness, the rain hit me, attacking my skin like a thousand little needles. It took my eyes a few seconds to acclimate to the low light. Then Tommy peeled out of his parking place.

"Tommy!" I shouted, running toward him. "Don't leave me alone!" He drove past, gesturing wildly for me to leave.

Standing in the dust of his car, I watched him drive away, confused why he wouldn't help me, especially after all the times I had helped him.

A roaring sound like a train engine barreling down on me caused me to duck. I kneeled and wrapped my arms around my legs. The train running parallel to the interstate wasn't scheduled for another hour, so the sound confused me. I had grown up with that train, listening to the piercing horn at all times of the day. This was no train.

I looked left and right, trying to find the source of the deafening noise, and finding none I glanced skyward. The underbelly of a huge jet came so close overhead the force of the air knocked me over, causing me to tumble several times. My hair blowing around my face, I followed the path of the blue and white jet. I caught a glimpse of the American flag on the tail. It was an enormous plane, bigger than any I had ever been on or seen. *United States of America* was emblazoned in bold letters on the side.

My mouth dropped open.

Time stopped.

The roar was deafening.

I wasn't aware of the gravel digging into my legs, or the horrific scene I had witnessed at school, or comprehend what was happening with the plane. All I could think about was the plane was the same one I saw on TV earlier this morning.

It was Air Force One, with the president on board. And it was about to crash.

CHAPTER 3

The plane sheared off the tops of trees and clipped a building, sending chunks of mortar and concrete tumbling to the ground. A strange object had been ejected, or blown off, and it shot high in the sky. I wasn't sure what it was. I lost track of it when a deafening crash filled the air with a fireball as tall as a skyscraper exploding into the sky, the flames erupted with billowing clouds of black smoke.

The stink of burning fuel assaulted my senses, and I covered my nose.

Then the shockwave barreled over the land, whipping tree branches like a tornado, and the force of it knocked me to the ground. I curled into a ball, covered my head, and thought this was how I would die. Alone, on a hard, cold parking lot.

Screaming in agony, I rocked back and forth as the pressure on my ears increased. I waited for death, to be released from this torture. Seconds passed, and the pressure finally equalized. When I opened my eyes, the school building was still intact. The trees, the cars too, and checking myself, I determined I was uninjured.

I guess it wasn't my time to die.

I sprinted to my car and shielded my face with my arm as the stinging rain bit and nipped at my skin. I could still hear the high-pitched sirens from the ambulances.

What the hell was going on?

STAND YOUR GROUND

In the safety of my car, I called my mother. There was no answer, and after a few rings, it went to voicemail. It made no sense why she wouldn't pick it up. The phone was right beside her on the bed.

Come on, Mom, pick up the phone!

Rivulets of tears streamed down my cheeks. I had to get away from there. Venturing out into the streets and onto the freeway, I found I-10 was the most surreal scene I had ever witnessed. It was a maelstrom of idling vehicles with drivers either slumped over, or hanging halfway outside their cars. I desperately searched for some sign of life or of movement. A lone survivor ambled aimlessly among the cars.

"Hello!" I yelled. "Can you help me?" The man took one glance at me and took off running.

I didn't know what to do, and that smell was still lingering.

What in God's name is that smell?

Then it hit me; I had to find May. The fight we had earlier didn't matter, and whatever we had quarreled about seemed so trivial and insignificant. Surely those wouldn't be the last words I'd ever speak to her. She was my baby sister and I had always protected her. I couldn't fail her now.

I was momentarily overcome with panic so paralyzing I thought I'd pass out. I kept giving myself a pep talk. *One more minute, one more minute,* was all I needed. *Keep going.* I concentrated on lowering my heart rate and breathing deep, long breaths. Tunnel vision took over and I blocked out the people lying in the street, some already dead, some raising their hands as I passed by, calling out to me to stop.

I realized now why the man had run away from me. He was in survival mode, like I was when I ignored the people calling for help.

A few other cars were still on the road, and some drove the wrong way, weaving dangerously in and around stalled cars until they could go no further. The drivers were as confused as I was.

I drove until I could drive no more, until I was hopelessly deadlocked in the massive traffic jam. I got out of my car, flung my backpack over my shoulder, and sprinted along the side of the freeway. By now, the cloud had blanketed the land in a dark haze. I took a shirt out of my backpack and held it over my nose and mouth. My eyes burned, my lungs hurt, yet I was still alive.

And if I was alive, it meant May could still be alive. I rationalized it might be a genetic reason I was alive, because I couldn't think of anything else. We carried the same genetic makeup, formed by a thousand chance happenings.

I stumbled along the road, blindly at times, feeling my way in a few feet of visibility. I tried my cell phone again, only to find the lines were busy.

Gradually, the dark gave way to a feeble light, enough for me to try to identify a pattern among the dead. I quickly theorized the cloud was like cancer that didn't discriminate in who it chose for a victim. I ran past cars containing the great melting pot of people who made up the city. Every ethnicity, age group, educational level, or socioeconomic status had been hit.

I must have blacked out, because the next thing I knew I was standing in front of May's school. I swung open the front door and walked in. A wave of seasickness struck me and the room wobbled as if it was on a rolling ocean. I kittered off balance and I held onto a doorframe to steady myself.

I stepped around the dead bodies on the floor, pushed open the door, and dashed down the steps onto stable ground.

"Ella." A faint voice called. "Help me."

"May, is that you?"

"Yes."

"Where are you?"

"Over here. Hurry."

I put my hands to my mouth and yelled, "Keep yelling! I'm coming!" I ran in the direction of the pleas, which were becoming fainter and weaker. I stopped and whipped my head, looking in all directions. Leaves blew all around in the cold wind. A plethora of students and musical instruments lay askew on the football field. The strip shopping center across the street sat empty.

Among all the chaos I spotted a tiny figure huddled against a wall. It was May, rocking back and forth, arms wrapped around her knees.

I ran to her, knelt, and cradled her head on my lap. She was so frail. "Are you okay?"

"You came for me," she squeaked. Her voice was raspy, weak.

"Of course, I did. I had to find you."

"I'm sorry," she said.

"What for? There's nothing to be sorry about."

"Don't be mad at me."

"I'm not." May's eyes, which had been sparkling and full of fire earlier in the morning, had become dull and glassy. Her eyelids fluttered, she

STAND YOUR GROUND

took a deep breath, and went limp in my hands.

"May? Maybelline!" My words choked in my throat. "You're my little Beanie. Remember?"

"I do." Her voice was as weak as a soggy kitten's.

"Listen to me. You'll be okay, but you need to fight. You have to stay awake."

"I can't."

I scooped her up in my arms and I was surprised at how heavy she was. I had to get help. The hospital was too far, the school clinic would be of no use, so I decided to go home.

I struggled to hold her and several times I stumbled, yet I never let go of her. If there were any survivors, I couldn't locate any. The sounds of the city had gone silent. It was eerie walking alone on the street where usually children rode bikes, mothers pushed strollers, and joggers made their daily running quota. Cars should be whizzing by, a soccer mom with a cell phone to her ear, a harried father rushing to work, delivery trucks, the thrumming of lawnmowers and leaf blowers, neighbors walking their dogs.

All gone in an instant.

I pushed the fear out of my mind to concentrate on my goal.

I had to get home, to get help for May, and I was determined to do it if it was the last thing I did because we were sisters.

Each breath I took was labored, my lungs clogged with the particles from the cloud. My legs were as heavy as if I was slogging through quicksand. My arm muscles quivered from holding May. The air was heavy and hot like I was in a steamy sauna. Yet I clung to the hope my home was within reach.

One more step, one foot in front of the other was all I needed to do.

My mind wandered and the tall trees swayed, the whispering leaves calling me to follow them back to a time when May and I were little, sitting on a blanket in the yard, playing make-believe. We laughed and sipped imaginary tea while nibbling our sandwiches under the dappled shade of a magnolia tree. The fruity aroma of the white blossoms filled my mind with the hope and promise we had survived, and we would continue to survive. A strange feeling overwhelmed me in the deafening silence of a city gone mute, and the more I fought it, the more I became aware of it.

Fear.

I was scared out of my mind.

Finally, I stumbled to the front door and placed May on the concrete porch. Fumbling around in my purse, I found my keys and opened the door. I fell forward into the foyer and collapsed from exhaustion.

"Mom?" I croaked. Taking a difficult breath, I said, "Help us." Too weary to keep my head up, I laid down, resting my cheek on the cold floor. "We need help, Mom..."

There was no response.

Several minutes passed, and once my energy returned, I willed myself to a sitting position. Although May was still breathing, she was fragile and vulnerable. I gazed upon her with the knowledge her life depended on me. I crawled on my hands and knees to where she lay, hooked my arms under her, and dragged her into the house, inch by agonizing inch. She groaned when her back bounced over on the threshold. I breathed hard from the exertion, not realizing how exhausted I was.

Pushing myself up, I stood against the wall, and, like a drunk, stumbled down the hallway to my parents' bedroom. I needed Mom's advice. I threw open the door.

"Mom?" She was in bed with the covers up to her chin, her arms crisscrossed over her midsection.

I tiptoed around the bed and sat down next to her. She looked so peaceful and quiet, her porcelain complexion smooth and untarnished from the ravages of her illness. I placed my hand on her arm to wake her. I gasped and immediately withdrew my hand.

She was cold, and I knew then she was gone. I was too stunned to cry, and even if I had tried, I had no more tears to shed. With great sadness, I pulled the covers over her face. I silently closed the door and stumbled down the hallway to the foyer. I slid down next to May, and with exhaustion overcoming me, I closed my eyes and drifted into a fitful sleep. Hazy images of friends and snippets of conversations weaved through my semi-consciousness. I tried to hold onto them, remembering their faces and voices, yet it was like trying to hold water in my hands. It slipped away, never to be reclaimed again.

I wasn't sure how much time had passed. Perhaps a few minutes, perhaps an hour. My eyes popped open and I rubbed them.

The shadows outside were long and dark, and the street was uncommonly silent except for the chattering of blue jays flitting in the treetops, searching for a place to roost. Mesmerized by the jays, my eyes followed their fluttering movements until a strange noise echoed in the stillness. It was a mournful, guttural sound akin to a large carnivore claiming a prized kill. It sounded like a lion.

STAND YOUR GROUND

I had noticed when a bird of prey alighted high in a pine tree near our house, the blue jays squawked loud, pestering the hawk by darting close to it, snapping their bills, jeering and mimicking another hawk, trying to force it away by alerting other birds of its presence.

Now the birds went silent, and the stillness of the house worried me, closing in on me like a coffin lid being slammed shut. The hair on my arms prickled and my sixth sense alerted me to predatory eyes. I sprang up, shut the door, and turned the lock.

Trembling, I put my back against the wall and slid away from the front door, keeping my eyes on the beveled glass decorating the door. I had no idea what had happened or why, but for now May and I were safe, we were together, and, as of now, it was all that mattered.

All the hurt I had experienced earlier when May and I traded barbs vanished as easily as a dewy raindrop in the blistering heat of the desert. May and I were sisters, and we would survive, no matter what we would face in the future, or what we had to do. The world was crumbling around us, people had died, and I lost the innocence of my youth that day.

CHAPTER 4

Central Texas
Fifty Years in the Future

I couldn't believe I had agreed to the interview. I had repressed those memories, and now I had to live them all over again.

I must have been a sight with my long silver hair blowing in the wind, sitting high on a horse. My hair went gray in my late teens, but considering what I had seen and done, it wasn't a surprise. I joke about my gray hair being the same as a gunslinger putting notches on a gun, signifying the number of kills. I did plenty of killing, accumulating more notches than would fit on a gun.

I sat straight in the saddle with my shoulders back, keeping rhythm with the horse's long-legged gait easily gobbling up distance. The zebra dun was making good time on our journey into the rural Texas community. My ranch was tucked away in the foothills of the Texas Hill Country, once covered by an ancient inland sea. Limestone fossils dotted the hills, and in my spare time I collected various fossilized sea creatures once inhabiting the great ocean.

"The Age of Dinosaurs" I believe it was called. Creatures with unimaginable strength and cunning who dominated the Earth for millions of years. A shiver ran down my spine and a feeling I was being watched

STAND YOUR GROUND

washed over me. I pulled in the dun's reins, her hooves quieting, allowing me the opportunity to listen to the sounds of the country.

The wind whistled around me, and I took in the feeling of the land and of the animals and for anything that might disturb its relaxed rhythm. I had learned to read the land as if I was reading an instruction manual. I had learned to rely on my sixth sense to survive and to notice anything out of the ordinary. It had saved my life several times.

A field sparrow flitted by and landed on a fence post, oblivious to my concern. Clouds floated in the sky, strung together like cotton candy, and I glanced skyward, searching the wide open blue for any hint of my real-life nightmares.

My hand gravitated to my bolt-action rifle tucked securely in the scabbard. I never went anywhere without it. I needed to be prepared if somebody or some*thing* tried to attack me.

It had been a long time since I had to kill a man, or a tearawolf, the mutant creatures created by man-made germ warfare. We called them tearawolves because I witnessed one tearing apart a man in a matter of seconds. I thought we killed them all, but couldn't be quite sure, and it was the reason I carried a rifle wherever I went. I also had a six-shooter and a knife for backup.

Because the winter rains could make an appearance soon, I was wearing a tan colored, weatherproofed poncho, and I'd learned never to be caught unprepared, to check my rifle and ammunition, to carry extra food and water, and to make sure my horse wasn't lame.

A rush of autumn hugged me with a teasing of rain, the life-force of the land, renewing the parched grass and the crops hungry for its rejuvenating qualities.

A wide sombrero shaded my skin, wrinkled from the sun. I don't mind my wrinkles, and wear them like battle scars. I had real scars. The longest one snaked down my thigh to my calf, yet I kept it hidden it because it brought stares and questions.

The sombrero was given to me a long time ago by a Mexican woman who had crossed the border into Texas looking for someone, anyone she could take care of; to latch onto, to give her life meaning after her entire family had died. She said she had always taken care of other people, and since she had nobody left, wanderlust called her away. I fed her and let her take shelter in my home, and I asked her to stay, but she said God told her it was not to be.

She called me Aya because she could never say my name, Ella. Some people still called me Aya. The woman stayed only for a while then left one day as mysteriously as she appeared. I had no idea what happened to her, or if she headed south to cross back over the border into her homeland. There were no more borders, only the ones in our minds, keeping us from realizing what we could do.

Those fluffy clouds had given way to wispy cirrus clouds high in the sky. A flock of Canada Geese honked in the wide expanse, wings flapping silently as they migrated south for the winter.

It was a gorgeous day to be alive, and a day like today made surviving all the hunger and pain and fear worthwhile. Life would find a way. It always did. There was a time when I had wanted to die, to give up, to lay down when I was wounded and bleeding, with not a soul around.

It would have been so easy to die, safe in my treehouse with memories of my childhood all around. I could have surrendered to the pain and the agony, yet I didn't, because someone dear to my heart saved me.

My horse slowed to a trot along what was once a highway. I discerned a pale yellow line in the dry grass, remnants of asphalt long since crumbled away in the blistering heat of decades of summers, but if you dug in the dirt, clumps of it still existed. Younger folks took it home to display over fireplace mantels, like a trophy or something precious.

I came to the edge of town, where a car rolled along the road, and children were running alongside it. I kicked my horse in the side to make her gallop so I could see the car firsthand.

It was a fine-looking car with sleek lines and a light colored leather interior, and at one time had all the latest bells and whistles—satellite radio, GPS, Bluetooth—all useless now. I recalled the same car on the road over fifty years ago when I was eighteen.

For a moment, I pondered how fifty years slipped by so fast. We think we have all the time in the world, until our time is up. I liked to think I'd spent mine well, and perhaps I'd left a mark on the world.

I had no regrets.

The driver slowed the car and waved as he approached me. He honked twice, the noise startling my horse, and I took up the slack in the reins to steady her.

"Hello, Ella! What brings you into town? I haven't seen you in a long time," Hank Witherspoon said. He was a generation younger than me and owned a junkyard. He collected all sorts of old rusty appliances, tools, car parts, anything he could find. He repaired a tractor for me once. Come to think of it, he could repair most anything, tinkering with it until he got it to

STAND YOUR GROUND

work.

"I'm going to be interviewed," I replied.

"What for?" His right hand was resting on the steering wheel, his left arm, bent at the elbow, was on the door.

"My life story."

"Well, Lordy be! That surely will be interesting. You've had one heck of a ride, Ella."

"That's a fine lookin' car you have there. Where'd you find it?" I rested my hands on the saddle horn. My horse moved in closer to inspect the car. Her nostrils flared at the new smells of leather, gasoline, and oil.

"I found it in a barn at an abandoned ranch about sixty miles west of here." Hank put the car in park, turned off the engine, and stepped outside. He steepled his fingers together, stretching his arms out straight. He bobbed his neck side to side, and it audibly popped. "That feels right good. Been bent over too long, staying up all night fiddling with the engine trying to get this beauty to work. She finally purred to life. Ain't she a work of art?"

"Sure is."

"German-made, don't you think?" Hank asked.

"I think so." Flashes of my teen years came to me. My mind receded to a TV commercial where a sleek car maneuvered effortlessly along a two-lane highway cut into a cliff, high above the sea where the waves crashed into the rocks below. I would have been sitting on the sofa in our family den, my dad reading a book in his favorite chair. My mom would have been in the kitchen, and May would have been in her room, no doubt texting a boy. A memory I hadn't thought about in years, and now it was as clear as if it was yesterday.

"Ella? *Ella?*"

"Hmm?"

"You've been a good friend to me. It's something I've been meaning to tell you."

I nodded to acknowledge him.

"I was a teenager when my dad died, and you took me in when nobody else would. You barely had enough food to feed yourself, yet you went hungry to feed me. Why?"

"You needed help. I couldn't let you starve to death or die in the cold."

"You could have, but you didn't. I owe you my life."

"Hank, you don't owe me anything." I was suddenly overcome with a welling of emotions I hadn't had in a long time. My breath came shallow and hard. What was wrong with me? I turned my head away and rubbed my eyes.

"Ella, are you okay?" Hank asked.

"Yes, I'm fine," I lied. "I have something in my eye."

"Alright." He looked down and scuffed his shoe in the dirt, perhaps embarrassed at my show of emotion.

I cleared my throat and asked, "Do you still collect things?"

"I do. I've been on a few salvaging trips." Hank looked at me quizzically. "Ella, you don't make idle conversation. What are you getting at?"

"Have you ever made it to the old cities? Houston, perhaps?"

"A couple of months ago I made a trip to the coast, and I tried to get into what's left of Houston, but the perimeter is fenced off. Big signs in red letters say Do Not Enter." He paused and took a breath. "There's not much left. The skyscrapers are all gone. Houses, buildings, schools. Gone. It's wild. Creepy." He shivered. "So why'd ya wanna know?"

"I'm here to meet with some young fella who wants to record my life story. I've always wondered what happened to the big cities. I'd heard a few stories, but never talked to anyone who had been back."

"From what people say, those old cities are dangerous. The zoo animals escaped and have taken over. Vines everywhere. Stay away from there, Ella." Hank stole a glance at me. There was clearly something else he wanted to ask me. "You were from Houston, right?"

"I was. It's where my childhood home was."

"You were there when it happened?"

"Yes," I said simply. I didn't want to encourage more conversation about the subject. Fifty years later, the pain was still as raw as an open wound: The last memories of my mother, the confusion, the primal need to survive. Soon I'd have to spill my guts to a stranger, all for the education of future generations. I patted my horse on her coarse mane. It soothed me to feel the warmth and the strength of it.

"There ain't nothin' to go back to," he said.

I'd seen that look before when people learn of my hometown. It was a look of pity and I didn't like it. Hank mercifully changed the subject.

"What's this fella look like? The one who's gonna interview you?"

"Beats me. I haven't met him. He's some young guy from the university. We're supposed to meet at the library at noon."

I shifted positions in the saddle. Georgia, my horse, had been inspecting the car as we talked. She nosed the car along the sides, leaving

STAND YOUR GROUND

smudge marks with her moist muzzle, probably trying to identify the strange metal object. I could tell she was getting itchy to move on because she always stamped her right hoof then shifted her weight restlessly. I patted her neck, my splayed fingers threading through her thick mane, leaving noticeable striations in her hair.

Hank scratched the side of his head. "I was eatin' breakfast at Mabel's Café this morning. Some new fella was in the booth next to me. I overhead him say something about being in a university. Mebbe that was him?"

"Perhaps."

He took a step closer and petted Georgia with long, languid strokes. He glanced up at me. "Times are changing, Ella. I worry about you riding a big horse. Suppose you fall and break a leg? Nobody would find you. How 'bout I find you a car, get it working, and give it to you?"

I shook my head and huffed. "I'm too old to drive. I've lived like this since I was eighteen. I can't change now. Besides, I've forgotten how to drive."

"It's like riding a bike. Once you learn, you never forget. But if you have forgotten, I could teach you."

"No thanks."

"Okay. I thought I'd try."

* * *

Old memories were here in town, some I didn't want to remember. Some good, some not, but I was glad the town was bustling with activity, with people milling around. Stores were open, children played in the streets, a dog barked.

I rode on until I reached the library. I glanced at the sky and shaded my eyes from the sun-glint. I reckoned it was noon by the position of the sun and the growl in my stomach indicating it was time to eat. For lunch, I had packed a sandwich from bread I made using wheat harvested on my land, and an apple I had traded for with another neighbor, plus a handful of pecans I picked from the orchard near where I live. For dessert I had a big piece of banana bread using a late crop of bananas.

Dismounting my horse, I tied her to a post under the shade of a massive live oak tree at the front of the library. The ground was dotted with acorns and a squirrel barked noisily at me, swishing its tail. I smoothed the winkles from my jeans and brushed off the trail dust that had settled on my shoulders.

CHRIS PIKE

The library hadn't changed much since the last time I was there. Even some of the concrete sidewalk remained, and I imagined I was walking on what would have been the parking lot. The bricks were the same sandy tan color, although the front door was different, the glass long since broken. People had looted the store, seeking the books not for reading, but to use the pages as fuel for fires, or a substitute for sanitation purposes.

The door creaked open and I entered the library, greeted by the musty smell of books.

To the left was Jessica Harbaugh, who claimed to be educated as a librarian. I doubted it, but nobody questioned her, especially since there was no way we could check. She was my age, and she was a survivor who naturally commanded my respect.

"Good afternoon, Cindrella," Jessica said. Her tone was formal, which was how most people addressed me. I was somewhat of a legend around there, a title I never wanted. I had escaped the ravages of ailments brought on by the germ warfare of The Event. Some suffered from a sort of dementia, remembering bits and pieces of their lives, with big holes missing. Like they had Swiss cheese for a brain.

"Hello! I'm over here."

I glanced in the direction where the male voice came from. A young man with round spectacles, diminutive in stature, hurried over to where I was standing. This must be my interviewer. He clumsily walked into a library cart, stumbled, and a few books thumped onto the wood floor. He bent over, picked up the books, and shoved them back into the cart.

He thrust out a hand to greet me. I removed my riding gloves, one finger at a time, then shook his hand. It was limp and moist. Our eyes met for a second, then he glanced away.

"I'm Cindrella Strong, but you can call me Ella."

"I know."

His lack of manners caught me off guard, and I stood there, befuddled. He pushed around some papers on the table, obviously unaware I was still standing.

"Where do you want me to start?" I asked him as he scooted his chair closer to the table. The squeaking of wood on wood sent a shiver up my spine. Those types of noises still bothered me. I cleared my throat in an attempt to make him notice me.

My interviewer glanced at me, and I gave him a motherly scold. His eyes nervously flicked to the right and left. "Oh, uh, right. Please, let me get the chair for you."

STAND YOUR GROUND

"Thank you," I said graciously while he seated me. He was eyeing me over, studying me, like I was some sort of exhibit at a zoo.

"I'm preparing my thesis on the early 21st century," he said. "I intend to compare the theological thinking of the 20th century and how it affected the decisions, which led to The Event."

He rattled on about how he had studied that time period, especially the years before the Event. His platitudes completely bored me.

"I've studied and I've pored over old school yearbooks," he explained. "I gain a lot of information from old pictures, for example, like how people stand, their body language, facial expressions, the clothes they wear. Things of that sort."

"That's nice," I said, unimpressed, my intonation flat.

He looked at my jeans. "I think I recognize the brand of your jeans advertised in old magazines marketed to teenagers."

Mr. What's-his-name was clearly unsure of his account. His eyebrows furrowed, and he lifted his hand, rubbing what little stubble he had.

"It's amazing the jeans have lasted so long, and they look practically brand new. The fit is good too."

He must have been thinking about how a mature woman can still wear jeans meant for a teenager.

"I work every day at the ranch. It's like having a four-hundred acre gym in the back yard."

"Oh," he said.

"Besides, quality is quality."

I didn't want to disclose to him I had dressed up for the meeting. It was only the fifth time I'd worn the jeans. I was old, but had been told I could pass for younger. I was still strong from working the ranch, tossing hay, and tilling the soil. My back was straight too, but in the winter my aches and pains reminded me of my age.

We sat at a large mahogany table. My hands glided over the dark, smooth wood, and I admired the pattern of the grain.

Mr. What's-his-name fumbled around in his backpack and took out a tape recorder. He set out a tablet of paper and two sharpened number 2 pencils.

After much prodding from the university heads, I had agreed to let him record my life story. Perhaps I'd be in the history books someday. A giggle escaped my lips.

"What's funny?" he asked.

"Oh, nothing." I dismissed his comment with a wave of my hand.

CHRIS PIKE

The chairs were uncomfortable, and I wiggled around trying to find a spot that didn't hurt my backside. In the corner of the library at the brightly colored plastic children's table, a relic scrounged up from a pediatrician's office, sat a mother and her unruly children. She shushed them to be quiet. The librarian stopped the click-clack of the manual typewriter to make sure the children noticed her disapproving stares.

I rather liked the noisy children. There was a time when there were no children. They were the favorite targets of the tearawolves.

"You can start your story anywhere you want to," he prompted.

"Alright, what did you say your name was?"

"Theodore Olson."

He was of Norwegian heritage. His last name translated to "son of Ole." I should have already guessed that by his ruddy complexion and blond hair, although his eyes were brown. Quite a few people of Norwegian heritage survived The Event. They were sturdy people who could live off the land on practically nothing, using what little soil they could find among the rocky ground. The cold didn't bother them as much as other folks. I guess it was in their genes.

"Theodore Olson," I repeated.

"Call me Teddy."

"I prefer Mr. Olson." I sighed. "Where are my manners? First of all, thank you for allowing me to tell my story."

"No problem." He let out a condescending laugh, shrugged, and flippantly said without looking up at me, "There aren't many old gals like yourself whose memories are still good."

I glared at him, heat rising in my neck and burning my cheeks. He was too busy fumbling with the recorder to notice his transgression. All my senses zeroed in on my surroundings. The whispering of the children became noticeable, their words as clear as if they were speaking into a megaphone. The clock ticked like a drum beating, echoing off canyon walls. The odor of musty books hit me full and strong. I locked eyes with Jessica, who was peering at me over the rim of her glasses, and her gaze bounced from me to my interviewer.

"If you insult someone, you should at least look at them."

"What?" he said with a perplexed frown.

I lowered my voice, challenging him to look at me. "Old gal indeed!"

"I, uh, I meant—"

"I know what you meant," I cut in, my voice tight and sharp.

He sized me up. He immediately recognized his mistake and shrank

STAND YOUR GROUND

down into his chair. He glanced at Jessica, pleading with his eyes for her to help him. She shook her head and flashed her eyes wide, indicating he was on his own.

"Listen here, sonny," I said through tight lips, "I've plowed fields, dug fence posts, and bagged a deer in sub-freezing weather when we had nothing to eat. I came close to dying once when a tearawolf attacked me, clawing at my leg, ripping through fabric and flesh." I took a slow breath. "Tell me, have you ever seen a tearawolf?"

He didn't reply. I didn't expect him to. He only sat there, his downcast eyes focusing on his hands.

I raised my voice an octave. "Have you?"

"No," he squeaked, then announced proudly, "but I saw one in a museum."

"Oh did you now?" My voice was slow and purposeful. "Were the six inch razor-sharp claws filed down so little children couldn't slice off their fingers? Were the fangs removed?" My eyes burned into him, the contempt in my voice palpable. "Have you ever been so close to one of them you could feel their hot, stinking breath? Or seen the excitement of the kill in their eyes when *you're* the kill?"

He did not answer me, and the silence in the room was deafening. The clock ticked, the second hand magnifying each stroke. Jessica stopped typing again. The young mother and her two children stopped their make-believe playing, and sat dumfounded, transfixed on me, their mouths wide open. The mother brought her children closer to her and whispered to them. Whatever she said worked, because those children didn't move a muscle.

I lowered my voice to a whisper. "Ever had to run for your life?"

"No," he timidly replied.

Rising from the chair, I paced like a wild animal caged too long. My hands were on my hips, and my poncho swung when I pivoted. The thumping of my boots on the wood floor echoed in the silent library, announcing my anger.

I skirted the table and moved closer to Theodore, my face brushing against the day old stubble on his face. I placed a hand on the table, the other on my hip. With the look of a scared rabbit, he moved to the right, trying to distance himself from me.

"Have you ever had to run for your life?" I asked again, this time quietly. "Ever been afraid if you made one wrong move you'd be ripped to shreds by one of those beasts?"

I glanced at Jessica, who was as mesmerized as the children were.

"Have you?" I whispered into his ear. "Do you want to know what a tearawolf can do to human skin?"

Theodore didn't answer, nor did he blink.

I lifted my leg and planted my right foot firmly on the chair he was sitting on. I bent over and slowly rolled up my pant leg.

"Take a good look. This is what a tearawolf could do to a human. Hideous isn't it?" With raw emotion, I commanded, "Look!"

Theodore's eyes were big and round, his breathing fast. Out of curiosity he took a quick peek, then grimaced and glanced away.

"I was lucky not to lose my life or my leg. Perhaps you can write about that!"

I edged around to the other side of the table opposite Theodore. His chest was rising and falling rapidly. Fear flashed in his eyes. I've experienced fear, death, hopelessness. Fight or flight. And I've done both.

"I could teach you a thing or two. I've seen more in my lifetime than you would if you lived to be two hundred years old. So don't you Old Gal me!" I slammed my hands on the table. He flinched at the demonstration.

"I'm sorry," Theodore said, his eyes darting around nervously. "I didn't mean any disrespect."

"Is everything okay?" Jessica asked.

I nodded.

"I meant there weren't many ladies your age I can interview who survived The Event."

I should have socked him right then. He couldn't have put up much of a fight. Physically I was bigger, and my silver hair and wrinkled skin belied my strength. Although he was younger than me by forty years, I could have taken him. His hands were smooth with nary a scar on them, certainly not the hands of a working man. Those who ride a horse, or build a house, or cut cedar with an ax. Handle a gun, put food on the table, or who can bury a child and not be afraid to cry about it. I admire men at whose side I can stand as an equal. Kyle was one of those men. I doubt Theodore ever handled a gun or cut cedar in freezing temperatures. I doubt he ever tussled with a strong woman. I had my fair share of tussles in my younger days. A brief memory of Kyle interrupted my anger, and I smiled.

"I'm sorry, Ella. Are you alright?" Theodore asked.

"Huh?"

"Are you alright?"

"Yes," I lied. My heart was pounding, and the walls and ceiling were

STAND YOUR GROUND

closing in on me, suffocating me. My chest was tight, my vision blurry. I blanked out, my mind a jumble of memories. All I wanted to do was run, but run where? Home? I racked my brain trying to remember where home was. The man sitting across the table from me was looking at me oddly. His mouth moved as if he was talking, but no words were being spoken.

"Where am I?" I asked.

"You're in the library, Ella."

"Who are you?" I asked.

"I'm Theodore Olson, and over there," he said, motioning with his hand, "is the librarian, Jessica."

And like a light switch had been flipped on, I knew exactly where I was. "Oh, of course. I remember now."

"Can I get you something? A glass of water?" he asked.

"No. I'm too old for this nonsense. This was all a mistake." I reached for my satchel so I could leave.

"Wait," Theodore said, rising from his chair. "Would you like some coffee?" he asked hopefully.

"You have coffee?" I asked incredulously. I sat down and put my hands on my lap. "Where'd you get it?"

"At the grocery store, where else? Coffee has been available for over a year." He squinted, giving me a puzzled look. "When was the last time you were in town?"

"I don't remember. I have no need to come into town. I grow my own food. The land has pecan trees. There are wild berries and grapes to pick. I hunt and grow crops." He must have thought I was some crazy old hag. "When I need something, I trade with my neighbors, but I haven't had coffee in a long time. You have coffee?"

"Yes," Theodore said. "Right here." He reached in his backpack and took out a brown paper bag. As he unfolded the top, it made a crinkly noise, and the aroma of the rich coffee beans wafted out.

"Do you mind if I touch them?"

"Not at all."

I ran my fingers over the smooth beans, so dark and luxurious. The muscles in my face relaxed, and the tension melted away as I inhaled the aroma. My breathing returned to normal.

"I'll be right back with hot coffee for you," Theodore said.

He headed to the modest kitchen tucked away in the back of the library where he rummaged for a pan. It might take him five minutes to boil water. Gas service had been restored in various buildings in the city I had learned from a neighbor. I marveled at the simplicity and ease with which he could boil water. At the ranch, it was an ordeal and I only boiled water over an open pit when I needed tea. It was a brew I made from dandelion leaves. I learned from experience the smaller leaves made better tea, while the roots were used for "coffee". But real coffee? I couldn't wait!

I guess Teddy wasn't so bad after all.

He returned with a large mug, a spoon, and a bowl. He placed the bowl on the table, and my eyes gravitated to its contents.

"You have *sugar*!" I exclaimed, my eyes wide.

"Only for special occasions."

"This is a special occasion?" I asked meekly, seeking approval.

"Of course it is." Teddy sat up straight in his chair and exuberantly said, "You lived through a catastrophic event which killed millions of Americans. You escaped and travelled across Texas. You had to learn to live without electricity or modern conveniences. You had no medicine. You survived, and you became a leader at a very young age. That's a story worth telling."

I dropped my head, trying to hide the tears forming in my eyes. I blinked them away. I'd pushed so many feelings away, buried them deep within my subconscious. I had to, otherwise I wouldn't have survived. Why had I agreed to be interviewed? I'd have to remember all the fear and hardship of those early days. I was so young when it happened.

Teddy handed me a napkin. I thanked him and dabbed the tears from my cheeks.

I wrapped my hands around the mug, taking in the warmth. Using the spoon, I slid a half teaspoon of sugar into the coffee, and swirled the coffee around in the mug, the spoon clinking against the sides.

I tapped the spoon twice on the mug to let the coffee drip away from it and placed the spoon on the white napkin next to the mug. Curls of steam drifted upwards, and I relished the aroma as the muscles in my face relaxed, the tension in my shoulders melting away.

I brought the mug to my lips and blew short, cool breaths on it. Then for the first time in decades, I tasted real coffee. It was a sip, and I let the flavor fill my mouth. Several sips later I was like warm putty in the hands of a child.

The smell of coffee reminded me of my home where my mother and father enjoyed leisurely breakfasts on Sunday mornings. Mom would cook a southern style breakfast of biscuits and gravy, and serve it on the backyard patio under the shade of a magnolia tree. The sun's rays would

STAND YOUR GROUND

peek over the tops of the towering pine trees, raining down warmth on birds singing their morning melodies, flitting from branch to branch.

I could hear my parents laughing and discussing current events, my mind taking me back to when I was a teenager. A time I didn't know was soon about to end.

Teddy flipped a switch on the tape recorder, and pushed it near me.

"You can start now," he said.

"My name is Cindrella Strong, and this is my story."

CHAPTER 5

Houston, Texas
Current Day

I woke to the sound of a bloodcurdling scream. Laying crossways on my bed, fully clothed since I was too tired to undress the previous night, it took me a moment to gather my wits. My first thought was that I was dreaming, or someone was screaming outside, then I realized it was none of those options. It wasn't a dream, and the scream came from within the house.

Specifically, my little sister's bedroom.

In the darkness of the early morning hour, I pushed the covers off my bed, went to the door, and held my ear against it. I stood there for a moment, listening, the hairs on my neck prickling. I needed a weapon, and the only thing coming to my mind was a knife. My dad's guns were locked in the safe, and he kept the only key with him at all times.

A large knife would do.

Opening the door, I raced to the kitchen and fumbled around in the knife drawer, searching for a knife. The biggest, sturdiest knife I found had a wooden handle and a seven-inch long blade. I held it firmly in my hand, edge side up, my arm muscles tensing. Like my dad had taught me for self-defense, I dropped it to my side, readying it for an upward thrust

STAND YOUR GROUND

to do the most damage to the soft and vulnerable section of the belly, rendering an attacker helpless.

On cat feet, I tiptoed out of the kitchen, hurried through the den, then down the hallway to May's bedroom where she screamed hysterically.

My adrenaline was pumping at full throttle, and I had already decided if I needed to, I'd kill to protect my sister.

I pushed open the door a crack, looking for what I imagined would be a big man brutalizing May. Her room was dark, so I reached for the light switch and flipped it on. May screamed and thrashed around on her bed, caught in the throes of a nightmare.

I stepped over to her bed and placed my hand on her shoulder, gently jostling her. "May, wake up." I rubbed her shoulder again. "Wake up. It's only a nightmare."

To my surprise, she sprang up like a tightly coiled rubber band, obviously recovered from the previous day.

"Are you okay?" I asked.

Trembling, May folded her arms across her chest. "I think so." She ran her hands over her arms, her stomach, her legs.

"What were you dreaming about?"

"I don't know," she said. "I was hot and having difficulty breathing, like someone was pushing down on my chest. She sobbed and hiccupped gulps of air.

"It'll be okay," I reassured her. "Come with me. Let's get something to eat for breakfast. What do you want?"

"Cereal is fine. What should we fix for Mom?"

A breath caught in my throat. "May, I need to tell you something."

"Tell me what?" she asked, puzzled.

"Mom, she uh..." I swallowed hard, "...she, uh, died yesterday."

"What?" May asked. "Don't tease me."

"I'm not teasing.'

May furrowed her brow in despair. She stepped over to the door and looked down the hallway. "Mom?" she called out, her voice cracking.

When she took another step, I reached for her arm, holding her back. "Don't," I pleaded. "She was already gone when we got home yesterday."

"Where is she?"

"In bed. I covered her with the sheet."

"Oh," she said. Her face turned red and her eyes were tearing, trying to process the information. "We need Dad. He'll know what to do. Where is he?"

CHRIS PIKE

"No clue. I've been trying to call him, but I can't get through."

"Ella, what exactly happened? I only remember bits and pieces. My friends falling and thrashing around. How did I get home?"

"I carried you here. I found you crying by the side of one of the school buildings."

"Who else did you find?"

I shook my head. "Nobody."

"How's that possible?"

"I don't know."

"We need to call somebody," May said. "We need help."

Before I could stop her, she bolted to the kitchen. I followed after her. She picked up the receiver of the land line and punched in 9-1-1.

"I've already tried that," I said. "There's no answer."

"There has to be," May said.

"I tried for hours. Nobody picked up."

May dialed 9-1-1 again, then hung up when nobody answered. She slumped down in a chair at the breakfast table, hung her head in her hands, her chest heaving with emotion. I went to her and put a hand on her shoulder.

"It'll be okay," I said, trying to console her. She burst out crying. I knelt and hugged her. "We're together and nothing else matters."

It wasn't the truth, but it was all I could think of to say to her.

* * *

For several days, we stayed in the den, afraid to venture outside after we dug a shallow grave in the backyard to bury our mother in. It had been hard, dirty work, and May and I took turns hacking away at the hard soil. When I thought it was deep enough, I wrapped our mom in the comforter from her bed and laid her to rest. I said the Lord's Prayer, then scooped the dirt on top of the grave. May picked a few white clover flowers growing wild in the grass to place on the grave.

Burying my mother made me grow up really fast, yet I still clung to hope our dad would make it home. If he was still alive, he would have moved Heaven and Earth to get back home.

At night I slept on the floor using a bedroll as a mattress. May slept on the sofa because she was too frightened to sleep by herself in her room. We turned on the TV every so often, trying to find news—local, national, anything, even a talk show. There was nothing, only static. I expected a

STAND YOUR GROUND

public service announcement about what had happened, hoping to find some direction, but none came.

We played cards to pass the time, or read books to keep us entertained, and when we tired, we watched movies using old technology of CDs, that were now a godsend. I had teased my dad endlessly about his love affair with tapes and CDs; though I'm sure glad he had a collection any movie buff would be proud to display.

On the fifth day, I made a hearty breakfast of scrambled eggs, bacon, and toast. May flipped TV stations trying to find some news. She had become obsessed with checking every station, hoping she'd find a working one.

On the seventh day, while I was in the kitchen perusing the pantry, the Emergency Alert System blared over the TV so loud I jumped and knocked over a glass of water on the counter. The incredibly loud sound of an out of tune electric guitar hyped up on steroids was hard not to notice. It was so loud, echoing in my brain and bouncing around, scrambling it I could hardly stand it. Then it quickly became one of the sweetest sounds I had heard.

I bolted to the den and stood in front of the TV, my eyes attuned to the snow filling the screen like black and white confetti being ground up in a blender and spat out. Breathlessly, I waited. The Emergency Alert System occasionally tested by interrupting programming, but this was the first time it had been used for a real emergency.

"May!" I yelled. "Come in here. Hurry!"

She raced from the bathroom to the den and stood next to me. "What is it? What's going on?"

"Shhh, listen," I said, pointing to the TV.

The snow-filled screen morphed into a dark blue screen with bold white letters announcing *This is a nationwide alert from the Emergency Alert System.*

Then an authoritative male voice boomed over the TV.

"This is a message from the Emergency Alert System. This is not a drill. A member of congress will deliver a message in ten minutes. The EAS gives the president, the vice president, the speaker of the house, or the next ranking member the authority to address the public during a catastrophe. If none of the aforementioned people are available to make the announcement, then a member of congress will. Stay tuned for an announcement. Do not turn off your TV."

"Is this for real?" May asked.

CHRIS PIKE

"I think so. Let's listen." I sat down on the sofa next to May.

For several agonizing minutes, we waited and watched the alert scrolling across the TV, the lettering boring into my pupils. When I closed my eyes, I could still make out those letters.

I was innately aware of how silent our world had become without the steady hum of voices. My parents talking, teachers giving instructions, laughter from children playing near our house, friends calling, text alerts. I had become so desperate for another human voice I started watching movies on our portable battery operated DVD player. I had teased my dad mercilessly when he bought it, and my mom had said it was a waste of money. When he dug that out of the closet after we had been out of electricity for several days following a hurricane, I didn't tease him anymore. He had put a card table in the middle of the den and moved the sofa closer so we could watch the movie on the incredibly tiny screen. It paled into comparison with our big screen TV.

So much noise was caused by humanity. The washer or dryer humming, the whirl of the dishwasher, the ding of texts, the AC clicking on and off, traffic, lawn mowers, weed eaters, electric hedge trimmers, the thumping of helicopters flying above our house, traffic. How could I ever miss traffic? Yet I had lived in it all my life. So much noise in the Houston metroplex, and now the city had gone quiet.

How could I live my life in silence, especially a life void of other human voices, even if it came unnaturally from the TV or radio? We had become so accustomed to noise, and now that it was gone, the world had become terrifyingly silent.

Our neighbors had disappeared and only once had I seen a man walking along the street. He wasn't looting houses, and didn't appear to be searching for anyone, yet I was too scared to run out to him to ask him if he knew anything.

A dish clinked in the sink and it brought me back to the moment.

Then the EAS sounded again. May and I waited in anticipation. There was no video feed, only those white letters ingrained on the TV screen.

"My name is...my name doesn't matter. If you can hear me you need to know the president of the United States of America is missing. The last contact was as Air Force One was departing Ellington Air Force Base near Houston. We have no confirmation if he is alive or dead. The vice-president, the speaker, and most of congress are dead. Do not rely on the American government to help you. There is no government. I repeat. There. Is. No. Government.

STAND YOUR GROUND

"It is estimated the death toll is in the millions. The Eastern Seaboard was especially hard hit. Without a working infrastructure and people to support it, disease and starvation will result in additional casualties. Canada and Mexico are affected as well, with reports of huge casualties. Reports indicate the United States suffered a germ warfare attack, and most everyone subjected to the agent released through a cloud engulfing the Eastern Seaboard and Gulf States died within minutes. If you hear this, it means you are still living and more than likely you have some sort of natural immunity to the biological agent.

"It is unclear how the cloud dispersed over such a wide area, but it is thought once the agent came in contact with water, it rapidly multiplied at a pace no one anticipated. The entire Eastern Seaboard was hit, including offshore along with the Gulf Coast states. Fishing vessels have washed ashore. Offshore oil rig personnel were not spared either. Cruise ships are idle. Planes have crashed. The electrical grid was compromised due to a lack of manpower, but nuclear power plants are safe for the moment. Once their generators cease to operate, there will be nuclear contamination. If you are in close proximity to a nuclear reactor, you must leave the area."

May and I sat transfixed on the TV, listening to the man speak.

"Sporadic reports from ham radio operators indicate the biological agent has affected some mammals, resulting in mutations. Reports are coming in, but cannot be substantiated at this time. If you see something you think is unbelievable, then believe it. Protect yourself at all times, and carry a weapon if you have one. If not, do whatever you must to get a weapon. Learn how to use it.

"Other than that, I have no guidance for you at this time. Shelter in place if you have supplies, or if you don't have enough food or water, try to find whatever you can. If you have a country home with supplies, I suggest you find a way there because the cities are no longer safe. There have been reports of roaming gangs attacking defenseless people, and at times killing them.

"That's all the information available at this time. If you hear this, God bless you. And one more thing. Don't go out at night."

I waited for additional instructions from the man, and when there were none, I looked at May, who had gone white. She had curled into a fetal position on the sofa, her arms wrapped around her legs. She rocked. I went to her and brushed strands of hair out of her face like our mother did when we were little and needed our tears dried. I took the afghan from the back of the sofa, placed it over her, and tucked her in like she was a little child. For a long moment I sat next to her, thinking about solutions.

Various scenarios crossed my mind, and I mentally checked each off the list as not being viable. Then it hit me regarding what I had to do.

CHAPTER 6

"May! Get up, May!" I jostled her until she woke.

"What do you want?" she asked groggily. "Leave me alone. I want to sleep. I can't deal with this right now."

"There's no time to sleep. Pack whatever you can carry on your shoulders. We're heading to the ranch."

"The ranch! Why? It's two hundred miles from here to the middle of Texas."

"Waco is close by," I offered.

"Waco sucks."

"No it doesn't. One of the most popular HGTV shows is filmed there."

"This was the last season."

"I don't want to argue about it. What's important is the ranch has all we need," I said. "Uncle Grant should be there, and we've got enough food for a year. The last time we were there I helped Dad and Uncle Grant inventory and stock the cellar, so I'm confident what's in there. Dad left a Winchester .30-30 in a rack upstairs, and there is ammo in the chest in the room, so I can hunt when we need meat. Dad also left a couple .44 Smith and Wesson pistols we can use if we need protection. Anybody who sees a .44 pointed at them won't mess with us."

"Those are big guns, aren't they?"

"It's what Clint Eastwood carried in the *Dirty Harry* movies."

STAND YOUR GROUND

"Can you shoot those?" May's skepticism was apparent.

"I can. Dad let me shoot it with light loads, so you'd be able to shoot it too. You have to hold it steady with a firm grip. It's easy to load and I can show you how. We'll be fine once we are there. The orchard has plenty of fruit trees, and wild grapes grow on the fence line, and I'll get the garden up and going, so we'll be able to supplement our—"

"That's all good and everything, Ella," May interrupted, "but how will we get there? We have no car. The freeway is impassable from what you said, and I'm not walking all the way to the ranch. It must be close to two hundred miles."

"We're not walking all the way there. We will only have to walk a few miles. I've got it all figured out."

May sat up and rubbed the sleep out of her eyes. "I don't want to stay here so what should I pack?"

"Let me think a second."

I made a mental checklist of the pantry and medicine cabinets at the ranch. Those were well stocked, along with the cellar. My mom never liked going grocery shopping when she was there, preferring to use her time doing things she liked, especially birding and identifying which local flora had uses other than being ornamental. If everything went well, it should only take us a day or so to get there.

I snapped my fingers. "I got it. Pack snacks for yourself, enough water for a two day trip, and several changes of clothes. I'll get the same for me, and the book about how American Indians used plants for medicine."

"You still haven't answered my question." May looked pointedly at me. "How will we get there?"

As I was about to answer her, the train running parallel to I-10 sounded its horn. Many times I cursed the train and how it made the windows rattle. I used to cover my head with a pillow to drown out the noise. As of now, it might as well been Beethoven's *Moonlight Sonata*.

It was the most beautiful sound in the world.

"The train. We're riding the train. That's how we're getting there." My voice rose in excitement.

"Trains are slow. How long will it take us?" May asked. "When Dad drives it takes him three hours."

"Right, but Dad speeds, and the train doesn't. The trip shouldn't take longer than six hours, but we still need to pack extra water in case something goes wrong."

"How do you know where it's going?"

"Don't you remember? I did a research paper on the train last year. I learned all sorts of good stuff about it. Like its schedule, its route, how fast it goes, what it transports, and the pollution it—,"

"Okay, okay, I get it."

"Come on," I said. "We've got exactly forty-five minutes before the train swings around and comes back our way. We don't want to miss it."

"I've got a question. When do you think we'll be able to come back home?"

I didn't answer immediately because I wasn't sure whether to tell her the truth. Squashing her hope would not accomplish anything, and I couldn't be mean to my little sister.

Mustering my best reassuring voice, I said, "We'll come back when this blows over. I'm sure it won't be that long."

* * *

Thirty minutes later, May and I were standing in the kitchen. I took one look, then decided at the last minute to stuff a silicon expandable orange bowl into a side compartment of my backpack. Once collapsed, the bowl's thickness was less than an inch, and it only weighed a couple of ounces. It might come in useful. I opened the back door, and a rush of East Texas humidity thick with a putrid odor hit me full and strong. I gagged, and put my hand to my mouth and nose to keep from hurling my breakfast.

It was the smell of death.

Of people. Lots of them. Thousands probably.

Sickly sweet and rancid at the same time, it made my stomach turn. I'd never forget the smell of thousands of bloated bodies, the gasses bubbling.

I jumped back in the house, surprising May, who stumbled back. I slammed the door shut. "May," I gasped, "we need several scarves."

"What's wrong?"

"We need to cover our noses."

"Why? What's out there?" she asked, trying to look past me.

Swallowing the bile in my throat, I croaked, "The smell of death."

"From the people who died?"

I nodded.

May dropped her backpack and hurried to her bedroom, where I could hear her rummaging through drawers, and opening and shutting closet doors.

"Hurry!" I yelled. "We don't want to miss the train."

STAND YOUR GROUND

She returned in a minute holding several brightly colored scarves, and one wool scarf meant to be worn in winter.

"I couldn't decide which ones were better," she said, holding up several scarves in her hands. "We still need to look good."

I burst out laughing. "Even in the apocalypse, you still want to look pretty."

She smiled. "Never know who you'll meet."

We took a moment to tie the scarves around our noses and mouths like outlaw bank robbers who made an escape on a horse. I wished we had a horse about now for transportation. My dad was never keen on us having a horse, saying it was too much trouble, and once May and I tired of the horse, he'd have to take care of it.

I'm not even sure why I locked the house. It's not like it would deter looters from getting in. Leaving had to be the right decision, I reminded myself. The water was only a trickle now, and the toilets stopped working several days ago. I hadn't seen a living soul in days. Odd noises at night kept me awake, scaring the bejesus out of me, and I had checked and double checked the windows and doors, making sure those were locked and secure. If there was a right time to leave, this was it.

There was no looking back now.

To save a few steps, we headed out through the backyard, which opened to the athletic field behind our house. Pine trees and oaks rimmed the perimeter of several soccer fields, a running track, and tennis courts of a local charter school. Beyond, a baseball field with bleachers sat empty, then a row of businesses lined the south side of the freeway.

The wooden fence had been recently built, and it was taller than normal to prevent errant lacrosse balls flying over the fence and breaking our windows. After several windows had been broken, my dad got fed up and had the high fence built. The only problem was I couldn't see over the fence, and what we had to face.

At the time the cloud hit, school was in session, students would have been practicing band, or first period track would have been out running, or high school seniors would have been on the tennis court. I dreaded the scene.

We were saddled with heavy backpacks, stuffed to the point the zippers wouldn't zip all the way around. To save space in the backpacks, we wore two shirts each, two pairs of pants, underwear, and socks. I even had a jacket tied around my waist. May went the extra mile, and was wearing a coat.

Glancing at her, I laughed.

"What are you laughing at?" May asked, shooting me *that* look.

"You. My little Beanie. You look like a bag lady who is wearing everything she owns. All you need are smudge marks on your face."

May bent down, rubbed her fingers in the soil, and swiped her hand over her forehead. "How do I look now?"

"Like a bona fide bag lady."

"Do you have any spare change for an old woman?" she asked playfully, using her best gravelly voice.

We both laughed. It was good to hear her laugh, and the thought I came close to losing her a week ago, scared me. How could I live my life without my only sister? We shared the same DNA, same childhood experiences, then we drifted apart, not able to stand the sight of each other. Now, we've come back together.

She and I against the world.

Our house was located about a mile south of the massive Interstate 10, consisting of twenty-six lanes which I nicknamed the Big Apple after New York City, because the freeway never slept. Cars sped by, even during the wee hours of the morning, and rush hour traffic was bumper to bumper. I always wondered where everybody was going. Always in a rush to get to the office, get home, make it to an appointment, missing life along the way. Now it was as quiet as a graveyard. Even the chirping birds had gone silent, which was highly unusual. I paused, searching for the flight of a sparrow, or the squawking of a blue jay. Surprisingly, there was none.

Dismissing the lack of bird activity, I tied the scarf tighter around my nose and mouth. If only I could tie it around my eyes so I wouldn't be subjected to the horror that lay beyond.

My hands trembled as I reached for the gate latch, and I steeled myself for the scene.

CHAPTER 7

I hesitated, disturbed by the low buzz filling the air. "May, do you hear that?"

"Like someone humming?"

"Yeah, like a hundred people humming. What do you think it is?"

"I'm not sure. I'm scared and want to stay home." May tugged on my backpack. "Let's stay here, okay? We can wait this out. Please, Ella."

I stared at my sister, considering. After a minute of silence I said, "We have to leave, May. We have no other choice."

"There are always choices," she said, brushing a fly away from her hair.

It was then I noticed a plethora of bees in our yard. Bees occasionally would buzz the flowering plants, but nothing like this. It was like they were consuming as much nectar as possible, fattening up for the winter. I filed the information away in my brain.

"We need to leave. As soon as we get to the ranch, Uncle Grant will be able to help us."

May glanced away, then hitched her backpack higher on her back. After a beat she said, "Alright. We better get going before I change my mind."

I took a deep breath to calm myself for what was coming. "May, hold onto my backpack and keep your eyes down. Do not look."

STAND YOUR GROUND

"Okay," she squeaked.

I glanced back at our house and tried to memorize the way it looked, the way it smelled when my mother cooked my favorite meal. I tried to remember the softness of my bed, how the morning light woke me, the sounds of doves cooing in the morning, the good times I had with my family. So many memories I needed to keep. I wanted to take it all in because I had a sinking feeling I wouldn't be back.

The gate popped open.

A sickening buzzing sound increased, and I was greeted by a cloud of black flies so thick the school buildings were obscured.

In the heat of the morning, I slapped away the flies from my face, bouncing off me like I was a window pane.

The flies were thickest around the bloated bodies of students, a flying pox on the land, fighting each other to be the first to devour the tender parts of the flesh.

A glint caught my eye and I looked in the direction of the buzz. A shiny brass French horn rose above the revulsion, untouched by the tragedy befallen on the people, an inert object, no emotions or sorrow, cold to the touch, yet when in skilled hands, music as warm as a spring day resulted.

I wish I was cold brass so I wouldn't have to feel or experience any of this. I took a step, then another, marching through the unimaginable scene, weaving my way around the bloated bodies where the forehead skin had started to pull away from skull.

I slapped away flies now becoming tangled in my hair, crawling as if I had a head full of lice. I picked up the pace. "May, are you okay?"

"Just hurry."

"I'm trying. Please don't look. Keep holding onto my backpack." I imagined having blinders on each side of my face, like horses wear during races to keep their eyes straight ahead, and from becoming distracted with their goal. With tunnel vision, I kept focused on my goal to reach the freeway. I plodded on across the soccer field, and when we came to one of the school buildings, I purposely hugged the outside. There were fewer bodies near the school because the students fell on the field where they had been practicing.

After several long minutes, I found my way to the tennis courts, then wove my way along the perimeter of the practice baseball field. The baseball team would have been practicing before school in preparation for the playoffs, and while the bodies were unrecognizable, I would have known many of them from the neighborhood newspaper. A group photo of smiling young men wearing baseball uniforms, all their names listed under the photo.

In a way, they were the lucky ones. Dead before they knew the horror the survivors would face. I noticed movement around a body. A pack of dogs was tearing at one of the bodies. A Labrador, a dachshund mix, a brown mutt, another Heinz 57 mutt, and to think only a week ago those had been pets.

They were snarling and snapping, tails tucked, wary of each other, yet instinctively seeking safety in numbers. It was survival of the fittest. Those dogs had reverted to a primal instinct to survive.

At last we reached the massive freeway, a jumbled mass of cars, trucks, delivery vans, and several eighteen wheelers, their engines long silent after the fuel ran out. Most drivers had died in their cars. Others had stumbled a few feet to die on the concrete.

I marched forward, and intermittently I'd pat May's hand to reassure her.

On each side of the freeway was a plethora of offices and restaurants, cut by side streets leading to the neighborhoods. As we approached the interstate, a man ran out of an abandoned Italian restaurant carrying a huge container of pasta. I called to him, hoping he had information that could help us, but he darted around the building and disappeared.

I approached an eighteen wheeler, and getting an idea, I stopped at one of the big rigs.

"May, stay here. I'll look for anything useful."

I held onto the door handle and hoisted myself up. The window was rolled halfway down, and I stood on tiptoes and peered in. A bottle of water was in the console, papers and receipts for various purchases strewn about the cab. Water would be a good find if we didn't have any, but what I needed was a weapon.

"May, keep a lookout."

I checked under the seat, behind it, dropping the sun visors down for any hidden objects of value. I opened the console and pushed around more paper, a plastic bag, a package of Kleenex–which I pocketed–and my hand came in contact with a hard metal object. I had hit the jackpot.

It was a .357 Magnum Ruger revolver. Not my first choice, and big for my hands, but it was better than nothing. I found two extra fully loaded speedloaders, so I pocketed those with the Kleenex and stuffed the revolver into my waistband.

"Ella! We have to go!" May yelled. "I hear the train."

STAND YOUR GROUND

I hopped out of the cab and we dashed across the freeway, weaving our way around cars. I easily navigated the concrete barrier, but since May was much shorter than me, I had to help her.

The train was getting closer, and the thumping and rattling became louder. It was the same type of train I'd seen at railroad crossings, the boxcars decorated in graffiti. Some hauled gravel or asphalt, cars, canned goods, sugar, grain, heavy equipment, even coal, scrap metal, and other large items.

The horn was loud, honking, a sound I imagined an enormous prehistoric Canada Goose would make.

May and I sprinted to the tracks.

The ground rumbled, and I was so close to the train, a rush of air hit me, blowing my hair around.

May yelled at me. Her mouth was moving, yet I was unable to grasp what she was saying. She tugged on my backpack, forcing me away from the train.

"You were too close!" she yelled.

The gravel surrounding the railroad tracks vibrated and danced as the train chugged along.

More graffiti blurred by, huge letters and symbols which had no meaning to me, yet such care had been taken by the artist to make the 3D images. I wonder what happened to those people. Where did they live? Are they still alive? Did it even matter?

"I'll jump on first," May said. "Watch what I do, then do exactly as I do. I'm going to put my cheerleading into practice."

May jogged at a leisurely pace alongside the train, me right behind her.

She was waiting, biding her time, watching for the best car, and I prayed like I'd never prayed before, hoping this was a good idea. One slip and she could lose an arm or a leg, and die right there on the sloping gravel bed supporting the tracks.

She stopped.

I stopped.

"Why are we stopping?" I yelled. I was winded, sucking in air.

"I have to catch my breath," May said, gulping.

More railcars flashed by, more blurred graffiti, until I was dizzy and lightheaded from the motion and the deafening noise.

"Now!" May screamed.

She sprinted alongside the moving train, her feet slipping on the coarse gravel, her arms windmilling so she could keep her balance. I mirrored her running, stumbling, and slipping, trying to gain traction on the gravel. She removed her backpack and threw it into an open car where it bounced to the side.

She lunged and took hold of a metal rung of a ladder, swinging her legs up and over into the open car like a pole vaulter. She landed on her feet. I admired her athleticism.

"Come on, Ella! It's easy. Pretend you're on the track at school and you've got to leap over a hurdle. You've done it a hundred times."

My heart was pounding; my mouth was as dry as a desert gully. It was now or never, and I gauged the space between the ground and the car.

"I'm not like you! I can't do what you did. I'm no good at flips or cartwheels like you are."

"Yes, you are!" she yelled. "The train is picking up speed. Hurry! Just do what I did!"

Without any further haranguing, I took a running start, dug my heels into the gravel, lunged, and tossed my backpack to May. She caught it, lost her balance from the weight of it, and thumped down on the floor of the car out of my line of sight.

My adrenaline was redlining, and my heart was pounding so hard I felt it in my throat.

I have to do it.

There was no looking back.

I took a big step, those huge metal wheels grinding and shrieking against the metal tracks. I lurched for the metal ladder and held onto it for dear life. My feet flew out from behind me, my body banging against metal and wood, and my feet dangled perilously close to those monstrous wheels.

May reached for me and yanked me into the railcar where I tumbled onto the floor, coming to rest on my back. For a moment I lay still to get my wits about me and let my eyes acclimate to the darkened railcar. Reaching up, I pushed errant strands of hair out of my face.

"Are you okay?" May asked.

"I think so."

"You're bleeding."

"I am?"

"Yes. Your face," she said. "You have streaks of blood on your forehead."

I touched my face then looked at my hands, stained with my blood. A wave of panic gripped me.

STAND YOUR GROUND

I can't be hurt. I have to be okay.

"Let me help you," she said, gently touching my face. "I don't see any cuts. Where are you hurt? Could it be your scalp? Let me look."

May pushed around my hair, searching for a gash, her delicate hands palpating my scalp. "There's nothing there."

I glanced at my hands. My fingernails had created impressions on the fleshy sides of my thumbs, and an inch gash where a trickle of blood oozed out with every heartbeat. "I didn't even feel this. Oh, wait. The ladder. There must have been a ragged edge or something. I guess I was holding onto the ladder so hard I dug my nails into my skin."

May unzipped her backpack, took out a bottle of water, and splashed some on my hands. "You don't want to get an infection. Try to keep your hands clean if you can."

"I don't have any bandages," I said.

A strange feeling overcame me and a shiver went up my spine. It was the same feeling I had several days ago. I scanned the interior of the railcar and it was then I discovered May and I weren't alone.

Sitting in the shadows of the car were three people, men more than likely from the outline of their bodies and short cropped hair. The patterned sunlight flashed across one of them, and I got a glimpse of a beard. I took a peek at May. She was as still as a baby fawn faced with danger.

Rising, I stepped in front of her to protect her.

"I don't have a bandage either," one of the men said with a slow southern drawl.

I couldn't see his face, or the man's next to him.

"But I do have a clean white T-shirt. I can make a bandage for you," he said.

He took a step from the shadows. He was tall, a few years older than me, and I didn't get any bad vibes from him. Still, it paid to be cautious.

"You don't have to," I said, eyeing him over the best I could, which wasn't very good at all, considering the shadows, the moving train, and the deafening noise. Then I realized he and his friend had been watching us the entire time, not even lifting a finger. I shot a death stare at them, my eyes boring into his friend sitting in the shadows.

"Ella?"

I recognized the voice. "Tommy? Is that you?"

"Yeah, it's me." He emerged from the shadows and dusted off his pants.

"What are you doing here?"

"I was going to ask you the same question."

"May and I are leaving the city."

"So am I."

"How did you think about the train?" I asked.

"The train report I did. Remember? We learned all about the schedule, what it carries, and—"

"I remember now. The one I helped you with."

"I got an A."

"You've been there the entire time and didn't help us?" My gaze bounced from Tommy to, to… The same height, facial structure, hair color, body build. "That's your older brother, right?"

"Yeah, Kyle."

"Why didn't you help us?" My voice was tight with anger.

"We weren't sure who you were, and we weren't about to put our lives in danger for strangers. Besides, you looked quite capable," he said.

"We could have been hurt or killed."

Kyle cut in. "You weren't, so let me make you a bandage. Your friend—"

"She's my sister."

"Okay, your sister is right about your hand. You don't want it to get infected."

My eyes bounced around, my thoughts a jumble of questions and possible solutions.

Kyle took a step towards me and squeezed my arm. I looked up at him, realizing he was a few inches taller than me. I had never been this close to a guy who I had to look up to.

"You're the girl who's been helping Tommy with homework, aren't you?"

"Yes, I, uh, tutor him at school." I glanced away, afraid to make eye contact, afraid our arrangement was no longer a secret.

"More like doing it for him. You haven't been doing him any favors by doing his homework."

"So? What does it matter to you?" I glanced up, defying him with a cold look.

Kyle whispered, "He was using you, like he does with everybody."

"Thanks a lot, big brother," Tommy cut in. "You've always had it easy when it comes to school."

"It's called studying. You should try it sometime."

STAND YOUR GROUND

"Whatever. I'm outta here. I'm going to check what else is on this train."

Once Tommy was out of earshot, I said, "That wasn't very productive."

"He always runs away from the truth or when he's challenged," Kyle said. He unzipped his backpack and I got a good look at what he had. Compress and clotting gauze, a tourniquet, scissors, ace wrapping, an IV kit, saline solution."

"What's all that for? Do you plan to help people?"

He gave me a cold look. "It's for me. In case I'm bleeding out, I'll need an IV."

His demeanor and matter-of-fact response startled me. On the other hand, he was being truthful. No pretenses or false promises. I appreciated his candor.

Kyle removed a white T-shirt. Using his teeth, he ripped the bottom seam out and tore a piece of white fabric into one strip, long enough to wrap several times around my hand. "Let me see your hand. I'm a medic. You don't want your hand to get infected, and you also need a couple of stitches. If you want me to, I can stitch it for you."

"You can?"

"Yeah."

"Can you deaden the pain?" I asked tentatively.

Kyle shook his head. "No can do. You'll have to grit your teeth. It's gonna hurt."

I reluctantly held out my hand.

"Have you had a tetanus shot lately?" Kyle asked as he donned a pair of gloves. He inspected my hand then poured disinfectant on it.

"I think so."

"Within the last ten years?"

"Probably."

"Good," he said. "Now hold still."

Kyle let my hand air dry, and holding a needle, he said, "This will sting."

He pushed the needle through my skin. "Oh my God!" I gritted my teeth and looked away. "Sting is an understatement."

"Breathe," he said. "Concentrate on your breathing."

"How much longer?"

"Hold on. I'm almost done."

I was so tense my shoulders were up to my ears. As soon as he said, "I'm finished," I relaxed a bit.

CHRIS PIKE

Kyle squeezed antibacterial ointment from a tube, and using his pinkie, smoothed it over the cut. He wrapped my hand, taking care not to make the bandage too tight. When he got to the end, he had already torn the fabric down the middle so he could tie it off. I watched what he did in case I ever needed to do the same for anyone.

CHAPTER 8

Central Texas
Fifty Years in the Future

I was sitting in the library with my hands in my lap, and I realized I'd been running my fingers over the old scars on the fleshy pad of my thumb on my left hand. I glanced at the rough scars, thin, crescent-shaped impressions made when I had dug my nails into my skin. In an odd way, it reminded me of my first meeting with Kyle, and how he helped me.

My hands were wrinkled and lined, and looked every bit of their nearly seventy years. They had witnessed the fall of civilization, the enduring hunger, and the pain of living. They had experienced the suffocating pain of losing a loved one, and the despair when I'd put a gun to my head to end it all. They had seen the rebuilding of a society, not the way it was, but into something new. They had also witnessed the victorious moments of my life.

It was confusing to me: the past segueing into the present so easily, as if it never existed, like sea foam made from waves crashing to shore and evaporating. Only my memories are left of that time, and frankly some of them were so appalling I had to file them far away, deep in the recesses of my mind, safe under lock and key so I wouldn't go crazy.

Opening the lock at Theodore's insistence has forced me to revisit

STAND YOUR GROUND

places I don't want to ever again.

"I'm sorry," I said.

"For what?"

"For calling you Theodore. It's so formal. I much prefer Teddy. You remind me of a young Teddy Roosevelt."

"I do?"

"Yes."

"But you didn't call me Theodore. In fact, you haven't said anything for a while," he said, scratching his head. "I've been sitting here looking at you, letting you remember. You've been miles away, reliving your past. It must be extremely difficult."

I sat back, studying him, the way his glasses sat on the crook of his nose, the angle of his jaw when clenched, the furrowed brow. He's so young, yet I was younger when I had to leave home.

"Please don't pity me," I said.

He shook his head. "I don't pity you one bit. Your story is captivating. Mesmerizing, in fact. I've never spoken with anyone who witnessed it firsthand. You're making history right now, Ella. Your story will be read by generations to come, and you'll live forever."

"I don't want to live forever."

"But your story will," Teddy said softly. "The things you must have seen are beyond my comprehension. Your will to survive and to persevere against hardships is difficult for me to wrap my mind around."

For a moment, it was unclear where I was, and who exactly Teddy was. He looked familiar, the way his jawline clenched at my previous scolding. His eyes too. They were educated eyes, ones which pored over books, digesting every word. He had studied the world. Perhaps not experienced it, but studied it. I guess he had been hiding in the comforts of musty old books, sitting on the floor in the darkened stacks where it was quiet and the shadows were short. It was never safe where there were shadows.

"You haven't experienced life, have you, Teddy?"

"Excuse me?"

"You've hidden yourself away from the world, haven't you?"

"I have no idea what you are talking about." Teddy glanced away, straightened his tie, and pushed it tight against his Adam's apple. He ran his hand over his forehead, brushing his hair away from his forehead, shifting his weight in the chair.

"You're avoiding my question."

"No I'm not," he said indignantly.

"You've used books to hide from the world. It's okay if you have. I would have done the same given the chance. I had studied sciences in high school, devoured the classics, and had planned to go to college to study art. I wound up having to fight to survive instead."

"It's the kind of education you can't learn from reading a book."

My gaze traveled past him, through the walls of the library, out onto the road and beyond.

My breath came in spurts and my heart was beating fast. I swallowed, my thoughts taking me back to the train and to Kyle and May.

It was loud. It was warm. My hair was blowing around from the wind rushing into the car.

I was sitting with my back against the wall; May had rested her head in my lap. I smoothed down her hair, stroking her face. My little sister who had the will and strength to hop a moving train was fast asleep, and now I was doing what our mother would do to comfort us.

My eyelids were heavy, and I blinked them closed, my body keeping rhythm to the train's movements.

The steady thumping of the wheels on the tracks, the railcars thumping and pitching, grinding, the sound of metal on metal had dulled my senses to the point of being so fatigued I couldn't keep my eyes open. Soon I drifted to sleep.

CHAPTER 9

West of Houston, Texas
Current Day

Groggy, I yawned and jerked my head up. I had been sleeping awkwardly, like an airplane traveler sitting in a cramped seat. I blinked my eyes open and became aware of the sound of the train. It was still moving and bouncing along the tracks past swaying trees, pastures fenced by barbed wire, livestock, abandoned cars and buses. A lone man walked along the road and paused when the train rumbled by. It was unclear exactly how long I had been sleeping, or how far the train had traveled. I caught a glimpse of a highway sign indicating Waco was still miles away. I hadn't realized how tired I was.

Kyle was sleeping, and I wasn't sure where Tommy had disappeared to.

My body was sore from sitting propped up with my back against a wall, and I felt the presence of someone close. I sat up bolt straight and in the process knocked May off my legs. She rolled onto her back. A man, the one who had said nothing when Kyle bandaged my hand, was trying to rip my backpack apart.

"Hey! What are you doing?" I said. When I tried to stand, he pushed me back down.

"Get away from us!" May shouted. "You have no right to—"

STAND YOUR GROUND

"I have every right to," he growled.

May shrank back away from him. She was no match for the man who looked like he hadn't bathed in weeks. His clothes were baggy, and it crossed my mind he could be hiding weapons under those clothes. Our eyes met, and I saw a vacant and dull soul, the kind of desperation a man has when he has nothing to lose.

I put my arm out to keep May behind me, then slid my hand under my shirt to reach for my .357.

It was gone.

"Is this what you're looking for?" the man asked, pulling the pistol from his waistband. "You're too trusting. Next time you and your pretty little sister should take turns staying awake."

He licked his lips, eyeing May in a way that made me cringe.

Anger boiled up in me, the same anger I had when an older and bigger bully picked on me as a kid.

With lightning fast speed, I kicked him with all my strength in the soft flesh of his groin. He grunted and doubled over, shaking off what should have disabled him. He must be jacked up on drugs.

His eyes blazed in anger, and he hissed, "I'll teach you."

In a split second, I gauged my chances of jumping uninjured out of the train. One glance told me it would be a suicide jump onto rocks and other debris lining the tracks, and I couldn't leave May to be brutalized by this man.

Kyle appeared out of the shadows, lowered his head, and charged the man, shoving his shoulder to the man's back. The .357 flew out of the man's hand and clattered against the wall.

Kyle bear hugged the man and they fell to the floor, rolling and kicking, a blur of two thrashing bodies. Kyle landed a punch to the man's jaw, his head snapped to the side, and I flinched at the sickening crack, like a tree branch snapping.

Kyle scooted away from the man.

For a few seconds, the man flailed around on the floor, his leg twitching, then he expelled a big breath and his body went limp. Satisfied he was probably not a threat any longer, I let out a breath I had been holding. I wasn't trembling, yet I had never been involved in a violent fight where lives were at stake. It was frightening to think this would be the new way of the world.

Kyle stumbled to a wall and propped himself against it. He stood panting, his face flushed, and sweat beaded his forehead.

"Are you okay?" I asked.

He blinked and nodded. "I'm good. Give me a moment." He leaned over and put his hands on his knees, sucking in air.

"Where's Tommy?"

Kyle shrugged.

I glanced at May, who was sitting in the corner, her hands wrapped around her knees, her eyes blank like she was in shock. She rocked, mumbling incoherently. Tommy was nowhere in sight.

Without making a sound, the man shot up, unfettered by the pain of what I thought was a fractured jaw dulled by a drug-induced high. He reached around his back and pulled a knife, the kind from an upscale steak restaurant.

In a blink of an eye, he crouched and lunged for Kyle, holding the knife low in front of him.

My adrenaline went from zero to sixty in a millisecond.

I didn't think or postulate, I acted to try to protect Kyle, who had his head bowed and was unaware of the impending attack.

I took one big step and shoved the man as hard as I could, but the force of his charge was far beyond my ability to stop him. By using every ounce of my strength, I distracted the man long enough for Kyle to realize what was happening.

The man was strong, and my reward for stepping in was being slammed against the railcar's wall so hard I crumpled to the floor like a discarded rag doll.

The man lunged again at Kyle, who shifted his body to the side and the man blindly swiped at air. Kyle levered his arm in front of him to take the brunt of the cut. The knife sliced open Kyle's left forearm, and blood stained his shirt. Keeping his injured left arm between him and his attacker, using his arm as a shield, Kyle continued blocking thrusts.

The .357 was feet away from me, so in one leap I stretched my body and retrieved the revolver.

I brought it up and sighted the man.

He was so quick, and with Kyle in the middle of the fray, I wasn't confident enough I could hit the mark.

This was completely different than taking my time at the shooting range, where the target stayed still and wasn't armed, or a carefully choreographed movie scene. This was real life with real time action, and Kyle's and the man's movements undulated, switching sides. As if the man knew I had the gun, he kept Kyle between him and me.

STAND YOUR GROUND

The man stepped back and mock charged Kyle, sputtered a laugh, then twirled the knife in his hand for intimidation.

For the first time in my life I saw pure evil, and it scared me.

"Once I'm finished with you, I'll entertain myself with these pretty little girls." He forced a belly laugh, trying to draw Kyle into a foolish counterattack.

It was then I viewed Kyle in a completely different light. Bloody and absorbing blow after blow, it looked as though he was barely hanging on.

My epiphany allowed me to see Kyle had blocked every serious blow after the initial strike. Though Kyle appeared to be slow and indecisive, he was allowing the man to tire himself out with ineffective, angry attacks. Kyle's eyes remained alert, looking for a final, decisive opportunity.

The man's confidence was starting to wane. He was breathing hard, his knife hand hanging downward, his body crouched forward. His eyes were wild and feral, ready to strike out in desperate fury.

Kyle backed up and pretended to slip.

The man took the bait and thrust with everything he had reaching for Kyle's stomach.

Kyle sidestepped left to avoid the thrust.

Following his forward momentum, the man rammed his knife into the metal wall of the freight car where it was stopped cold, and since there was no guard on the knife, his fingers slid over the blade, slicing the skin and tendons, rendering his hand useless. Stunned, he glanced at his bloodied hand and uttered a high pitched shriek.

Kyle rushed forward, gripped the man by his shirt collar, and slammed his head into the metal wall, forcing his face over the sharp welds holding the sheet metal together. Kyle punched the back of the man's neck with each fist before backing away out of reach.

Now bloody and badly hurt, the man still showed no sign of giving up. He switched the knife to his good hand. "I'll make you pay for this!" he roared.

Perhaps it was the thought of what could be in store for May or myself, or the knife glinting in the sun's rays, but whatever it was, the paralyzing fear I had earlier vanished, throttling me into action. In one deft movement I brought up the .357, held it tightly with both hands, and sighted it squarely at the man, center mass. I pulled the trigger, slowly, deliberately. The hammer came backwards, then released with the sight picture still perfectly centered on his heart.

The resulting simultaneous explosion and the thud of lead tearing flesh didn't bother me one bit. He had insulted me, my sister, and was tormenting Kyle. He clearly intended to kill everyone at his first opportunity. His irrational mind put all our lives at risk. I had to do something. I had to protect us.

The man stumbled, his eyes rolled back, and he slumped to the floor.

I kept my aim on the man in case he was playing possum like before.

"Is he dead?" I asked Kyle.

"Let me check. If he moves, be sure not to accidentally shoot me."

"I won't."

Even if he was alive, I had no intention of helping him. He could bleed out.

Kyle tentatively approached the man. A river of crimson bubbled out of his chest and onto the floor. Using his boot, Kyle nudged the man. He got no response, so he used the toe of his boot to nudge the man's cheek. Still no response. Kyle reached down to him.

"What are you doing?" I asked.

"Checking if he is breathing." Kyle put two fingers to the man's carotid artery, on the side of his neck. After a few moments, Kyle stood and shook his head. "He's gone."

"What should we do with him?"

"Toss him out."

"I'll help you."

"I will too," May offered.

"Be careful not to get any blood on your hands or clothes," Kyle said. "We still don't know if whatever killed everyone is contagious through bodily fluids." He glanced at me then at May. "Did either of you get any blood spatter on you?"

"I don't think so," I said.

"May? Did you," he asked.

She glanced away before she answered. "No. Do you have a first aid kit in your backpack? You're hurt."

"Where?" Kyle asked.

"On your arm. Don't you feel it?"

"I do now," he said, looking at his arm. "There should be butterfly closures in the first aid kit. I'll need some."

"I'll find them," May said.

I took a scarf from my pocket, folded it, and put pressure on his wound.

Digging around in Kyle's backpack, May found the first aid kit and a semi-automatic pistol. "You had a pistol all this time?"

STAND YOUR GROUND

"I did."

"Why didn't you use it?"

"There was no time, May."

I cleaned and patted the wound dry, then Kyle took the butterfly stitches and we worked together to carefully line up the edges of the wound starting in the middle. We placed the strips on one side of the cut, then gently brought the other side towards it and closed the cut.

After we tended to Kyle's arm, we sat down to recover from the ordeal. I sipped on water to calm myself, then handed the bottle to Kyle. He took a gulp and passed the bottle to May.

Fifteen minutes later, after our adrenaline rush had waned, we decided to toss the dead man off the train.

Kyle held his arms by using his long-sleeved shirt as a grip. May and I each took a leg. He was heavier than we expected and the center of his body dragged along the floor. Dead weight was always heavier. With great effort, we moved him parallel to the opening of the car. It was then I noticed the train had slowed, although for what reason I wasn't sure. I didn't recall the train stopping anywhere along the tracks. Trains came and went along this railway track for as long as I can remember, and while they slowed down for crossings, there was not a reason to slow down now, nor to stop, and this train was stopping.

"We need to get him off the train now," I said. "By the time the train stops, we'll be half a mile down the road."

"I'm going to count. We'll pitch him off on three."

May and I struggled to get enough lift on the man. Since I was taller, I stood closer to the open edge of the car.

"Ready?" Kyle asked.

"We're ready."

The man's head hung lifelessly and bobbed when we moved him. His eyes were open, his mouth frozen in mid-speech. Kyle had a tight grip on his forearms, which pulled his shirt out, exposing his belly covered with red trails of blood. I grimaced.

"One," Kyle said.

We swung the man forward then back.

"Two."

I struggled to gain momentum.

"Threeee!"

Using all my strength, and with my left foot planted securely, I heaved him as far out of the railcar as I could. Kyle and May did the same, and we simultaneously released our grip. I watched his lifeless body tumble awkwardly, arms and legs splayed in different directions. The corpse landed on the coarse gravel, then plummeted down the embankment.

I never forgot him, for it was the first time I killed a person.

It wouldn't be my last.

CHAPTER 10

Exhausted from the fight and the struggle to move the man's body, I sat down with my back to a wall, pulled my knees up to my chin, and hugged my legs. May sat next to me.

Tommy reappeared and gave us a once over. "What happened?" he asked, swinging into the car. "And whose blood is on the floor?"

"That man who was here was up to no good. Kyle got into a knife fight with him."

"Are you hurt, Kyle?" Tommy asked.

"I'll be alright. Ella was the one who finished him off. She shot him."

"Really? That's impressive. I guess I need to get on your good side. Too bad I missed all the action."

"Did you find any food?" I asked.

"No. Just a bunch of useless stuff." Tommy shuffled over to a far wall of the car and sat down. "If you don't mind, I'm going to catch a few winks of shuteye."

I didn't want to look at anyone, and fortunately nobody said a thing for a long time. Kyle had slumped down on the opposite wall, May and I the other one. Only one side of the railcar was open, and I was thankful for the noise the train made. Silence would have been too much at this point. It was like the noise kept us from talking or analyzing what we had done, and kept us sane during an insane moment.

STAND YOUR GROUND

"Kyle?" I finally asked. "Where do you plan to go?"

"Somewhere away from here. The city is starting to stink with all the corpses around. From reports I heard, other cities are as bad if not worse. People who are left are desperate for food and water. Two days ago, I checked out the grocery store."

"What was it like?"

Kyle grimaced. "Flies everywhere. Corpses. I covered my mouth and took as many canned goods I could carry."

Kyle retrieved two cans of peaches from his backpack, and my mouth watered. Although I was thinking he would offer a can to May and I, to my surprise he took a pair of socks, knotted the ends, put a can in each one, then knotted the other side.

"What are you doing?"

"Making you and your sister a weapon."

He stood and swung the sock in a circle over his head, and I watched in fascination. Then I understood.

"I can hit someone with it."

"Bingo. Especially if you don't have a weapon at hand, or for instance if someone takes your weapon when you are sleeping. Ella, you should always keep your gun hidden."

"I will." I glanced down shamefully, then lifted my gaze to meet his. "You should keep yours handy."

"Fair enough. We all make mistakes. I doubt either one of us will make the same mistake again."

"I won't."

"Here." He handed a sock-covered can to me, and gave the other to May. "Practice with it. Swing it like you're roping a calf."

"I've never roped a calf," I admitted.

"Doesn't matter. Just do what the cowboys do at the rodeo."

* * *

May and I practiced our moves by swinging the sock-covered cans like they were whips, except we didn't flick it at the end. I didn't want the can accidentally hitting me in the arm since the last thing I needed was a broken bone.

The train wasn't traveling fast at all, and was sure I could pedal a bike faster. Intermittently, the train sped up, and then slowed to a crawl again. This pattern went on for about thirty minutes. After tiring of practicing, I sat down, stretched my legs out, and tried to catch a nap. Considering all the excitement, it was impossible.

The rumble in my stomach reminded me to eat. I fished out a granola bar from my backpack, and handed half to May. Finding another one, I asked Kyle, "Would you like this one?"

"You keep it for yourself."

"If he doesn't want it, I'll take it," Tommy butted in.

"On second thought, I'm keeping it." I held the granola bar I was eating between my teeth then tucked the unwrapped bar deep inside my backpack.

Tommy huffed.

"Next time, try helping someone," I said, finishing the last bite of the bar. "They might help you in return."

"Which is what I did when you needed my help in third grade."

"You've held that over my head for years."

"But look what it got you…an invitation to all the cool parties."

"It doesn't matter anymore."

Tommy shrugged. "It used to."

"Things have changed, Tommy. Get used to it."

He huffed again and turned his back to me.

"Tommy?"

"I don't want to talk about it. Give it a break, Ella." Tommy pulled his cap over his ears, clearly a sign he had left this conversation.

"Kyle, what else do you know?" I asked. "You were telling me about the grocery stores earlier. Do you think we might try to scavenge anything from them?"

"I wouldn't bother. If you have a place to go to, hunker down there, ration your food, and if you can, hunt for meat."

"That's my plan."

"Good," he said. "Do you have a water source?"

"A well on the land."

"Excellent, because the water in the grocery stores is all gone."

"I figured as much. The faucets at our house were down to a trickle."

"Same at my house."

"Have you had any trouble in your neighborhood?" I asked.

"There was a gang of five armed men and one woman in our neighborhood going house to house. They had a wheelbarrow to take away canned goods and anything else of value they could carry out. When they got to my house I opened the front door with a shotgun pointed at who I thought was their leader. I told him he had to the count of three to leave."

"What happened?"

"He left on two."

I chuckled.

We sat in silence, listening to the knocking of the train and taking comfort in the fact we would be out of the city soon. Since the city had gone quiet, it had become too eerie, and I couldn't stand it anymore. My mind drifted to the ranch house we were headed to, and though it was empty and quiet, that was the way the country should be. It never scared me; rather it invigorated and nurtured my soul in ways I didn't always appreciate.

The train had slowed down to a crawl. I chalked it up to the conductor slowing down for a crossing, or possibly debris on the tracks. Whatever the reason, it didn't concern me much.

It occurred to me Tommy and Kyle, two brothers less than ten years apart, couldn't be more different. Physically they were similar, with the same athletic build, thick hair, and a sharp jawline. Tommy used people, while Kyle helped people, and I wanted to know more about him.

"What about your mom and dad?" I asked.

Kyle glanced away, probably lost in some memory of his parents, then he lifted his gaze and made direct eye contact with me. It unnerved me, and I quickly averted my eyes before coming back to him. I wasn't sure why, other than I hadn't expected him to look directly at me.

"When they didn't come home, I went to the office where they both worked. The roads were too clogged with abandoned vehicles, so since they weren't too far away, I walked." He shrugged. "It only took me about thirty minutes to get there, but once I was in the building, let me tell you, it was creepy, and I got the feeling I was being watched."

"By what?"

"I couldn't tell you, only that shivers went up and down my spine."

"I had the same feeling at home," I said.

"About being watched?"

"Yeah. And I heard some weird sounds at night."

"What did it sound like?"

"Like a lion roaring over a kill."

He passed his hand over the stubble on his beard.

"It scared me half to death."

It was a moment before he began talking again. He shifted his position and uncrossed his legs.

"I'm sorry I asked about your parents," I said. "I didn't mean to pry."

"It's alright," he said, letting out a shaky breath. "I found them at their desks, slumped over. There was nothing I could do so I placed them on the floor next to each other. They were already stiff…"

Kyle's face flushed, and I could have sworn he was about to cry. There he was, a young man in the prime of his life, recently discharged from the Navy, full of youthful bravado with shoulders that had carried those that needed carrying, and he was about to cry. I didn't mind if he did, although I didn't want him to feel embarrassed about it.

I asked a question to bring him back to his story. "What did you do?"

"I took a few jackets and covered their bodies."

He stopped talking and looked at the countryside. A few cows munched idly in the pasture, and a lonely donkey stood in the shade of an oak tree. A field sparrow flitted from tree to tree, and a breeze drifted into the railcar, offering a brief cooling comfort I was thankful for. Things weren't as bad if your body was cooled by fresh air.

"There was nobody left alive in the office."

"I'm sorry to hear what happened."

Kyle nodded. He glanced away and cleared his throat.

"Where were you—"

"Give me a moment," he said. "I need a moment."

"Okay."

May, who had been listening to our conversation, shook her head, and put her hands up, indicating she had no idea what to do.

It was quiet in the railcar. The wheels had ceased their squeaking and grinding on the metal rails.

Kyle lowered his head and took a deep breath, then another and another. For the next few minutes, he did nothing else other than breathe. He didn't open his eyes, shuffle his feet, talk, and didn't appear like he was aware of his surroundings. Then he lifted his chin, his eyes meeting mine.

"Are you okay?" I asked.

"Yeah."

"Do you mind if I ask what's going on in your mind? You looked a million miles away."

"I was breathing. We were taught in training to concentrate on our breathing when we're under extreme stress."

"Does it work?"

He nodded. "It does."

STAND YOUR GROUND

"Kyle, where were you when it happened? Did you see the cloud? I thought it was storm clouds from a tropical storm."

"I didn't see anything. I was at home, sleeping. My EMT shift ended a little before seven in the morning because my replacement got to work early. He told me to go home and get some sleep. It had been a bad night with a car accident and we were the first on the scene. Some poor kid probably lost his leg."

"You think the hospitals are still open?"

Kyle shook his head. "After I left the office building, I headed to the nearest hospital to see if I could help." He hung his head. "God, it was so bad in there. Dead people in the emergency room had been stacked up against a wall. They were covered in sheets. I almost vomited because of the smell."

I gulped and put my hand to my mouth. "It must have been awful."

"It was."

A noise outside caught my attention. "Someone's coming," I whispered.

Kyle shot a worried glance at me, then to May, who had pressed herself into the corner. There was no place to hide. I readied my .357, as the running footsteps came closer.

"Hello. Anybody there?" a man's voice called out.

Then he poked his head around the corner and eyed the three of us. I estimated he was about fifty. He had on a pair of jeans, a checkered shirt, and a cap with the logo of the train. He appeared none too pleased to find us here.

"Who are you?" I asked.

"You're on *my* train, so I ask the questions." He heaved himself into the car. "Besides, you're stowaways."

"We're only here for the ride," Kyle said.

"Who are you?" the man asked.

"Kyle Collins." Rising, he extended a hand to shake. "And that's my brother Tommy."

"Travis Richards. I'm the conductor for this train and you are trespassing."

I exchanged worried looks with Kyle and May.

Tommy yawned and stood. He kept quiet, not bothering to introduce himself.

"We're trying to get out of the city," Kyle said. "When the train came by, it looked empty, so we got on. We don't mean anybody any harm, and we certainly aren't about to steal anything. I'm escorting these ladies to their destination."

"Where's that?" Travis asked.

"As close to Clifton as we can get," I answered.

"That's west of Waco. I can get you there, but I've got an injured man who needs medical attention. Is anyone here a doctor or nurse? You two ladies look kinda young. What about you, Kyle?"

"I was a medic in the Navy. Got discharged, and now I'm an EMT. Can I help?"

"You can. Come with me."

"I can help too," I said. "I took a first aid class at school."

"That's more than I've got," Travis said. "Whatd'ya say your name was?"

"Ella Strong."

"You can come with us also." He glanced at May. "You two sisters?"

I nodded.

"And her name is?"

"May."

"As in April, May, or June?"

"No!" May butted in, her eyes alight with fire. "It's short for Maybelline. And I'm in no mood for any makeup jokes, okay? And I'm not a calendar girl either. I've dealt with those lame jokes all my life, and I've had enough. Got it?"

Travis took a good, long look at her, their eyes meeting in spirited disagreement, and I thought he might cuss her a good one. "You've got spunk," he said instead. "It's pint sized spunk, but spunk nevertheless. I like spunk. Besides, I don't mess with young ladies who have their hands on their hips like you do now. That means business. So, Maybelline, I'd be honored for you to accompany us to the front of the train."

"I'm sorry," May mumbled. "I didn't mean to lash out at you. With all that has been going on…our mom didn't make it. Our dad probably didn't either."

"No need to apologize. Ladies first," Travis said, sweeping his arm in the universal gesture asking us to go first.

* * *

May and I took the lead. Kyle, Tommy, and Travis followed behind. After we had passed a few cars, Travis decided it would be safer for him

STAND YOUR GROUND

to lead, so he stepped in front of us.

Travis walked purposefully, each step placed as if he had walked alongside a train all his life, which I suppose he had for most of his adult life. He wasn't a big guy, but he was muscular, like he might have been a running back, built for short bursts of speed, barreling over his opponents. Being a train conductor suited him. He took a moment to check the connection between cars, grunted a few words, then strode on.

My curious nature got the best of me. "Why did the train stop?"

"There was debris on the tracks," Travis said.

"I don't quite understand. Considering your line of sight might be a mile or less, how did you stop the train in time?"

"We had a new navigational system installed last month to alert us to any obstacles on the tracks. It allowed me enough time to stop the train."

"Right. Satellite technology and such. We've been learning about it in school."

"Something like that," Travis said.

On each side of the tracks were brambles of thorny dewberry vines, dotted with berries the color of a midnight sky. A butterfly flitted over the tops of the few remaining white blossoms, landed on one, then effortlessly glided away when we got too close.

"May," I said, "do you remember when Mom and Dad used to take us to pick dewberries, and how we were afraid one of our friends would see us on the side of the road?"

"Yes," she said, laughing. "I also remember all the bugs and fire ants, and that time I nearly stepped on a water moccasin."

I snickered. "You were lucky you didn't."

"Dad said the snake was probably after the mice attracted to the berries. Remember how Mom would make a dewberry pie for us, topped with Blue Bell vanilla ice cream? I sure could use some ice cream about now."

Looking at all those plump dewberries by the tracks gave me an idea. "Hey, guys. Do you mind if we pick some of these berries? It might be a while before we get fresh fruit again."

"There's no time," Travis barked, without looking back at me. "A man in the engine room needs help."

His demeanor brought me back to the reality of our dilemma. This wasn't a social occasion with our family where we could be happy and pick dewberries, then go home and take a nice hot shower to wash away the dirt and sweat on our bodies.

This was a life or death situation. The apocalypse...a scenario I didn't want to come to terms with. I wanted to remember my family and the laughter we once had. The four of us, happy, content. A hot shower and fresh water whenever we needed it, a full refrigerator, ice, ice cream, TV, radio, texting, music, friends, football games, the drama class. Friends.

My friends.

Time spent texting them about all the high school drama, who was dating who, who made bad grades, who cheated on a test.... My eyes flicked to Tommy. I had singlehandedly helped him get through high school by doing his homework, helping him on tests, and for what? A promise he'd take me to the movies or to a dance. What difference did it make now? My opinion of him had changed since the last time I had seen him. I was a silly school girl who had been blinded by infatuation. He had done one nice thing for me when I was too shy to take up for myself, resulting in me being indebted to him forever.

I still couldn't believe he had left me standing in the parking lot of school when people were dying around us, and what did he do to help me? Nothing. To make matters worse, he hadn't lifted a finger to help May or I when we hopped on the train, but his brother had.

A total stranger had helped me, and didn't want anything in return.

My reminiscing was cut short when we approached the engine. Pushed to the side of the tracks was the strangest...well, I wasn't sure what it was. A smooth, aerodynamic structure in the shape of a truncated cone, possibly even some type of new weapon. It was windowless except for two slits, with a parachute attached to it. The parachute lay tangled in the bushes, and it reminded me of the kind fighter jets probably used when landing on naval carriers. The hatch was open so I looked inside. There were two seats with harnesses, a survival suit lay crumpled on the floor, food wrappers had been tossed about, and the front had a panel that could rival the cockpit of a 747 or at least those in the movies. Instruction manuals lay askew on the floor.

"What is it?" I asked. "Travis, was that the debris you mentioned?"

He nodded. "I wasn't quite sure what it was. I needed to move it, and since it was teetering on the tracks, I gave it a heave and pushed it off. A man yelled from inside, so I opened the hatch to find an injured man. He was talking nonsense, saying his head hurt, and he was thirsty. He's the one who needs help."

I took one glance back at the pod, then hoisted myself up into the engine room.

A man dressed in a torn suit, his gray hair disheveled, purple bruising

STAND YOUR GROUND

on his cheeks, black oxfords covered in dust, his tie loosened, was sitting on a cot. At first he looked like a homeless man, yet he appeared to be physically fit, about six feet tall, broad shoulders, and his shirt and suit surely hadn't come off the rack. His suit fit like it had been tailor made for him, and his tie was quality also. He stood, and wobbled, yet he had an unmistakable air indicating he was an important man, one who was used to giving orders.

The longer I looked at him, the more I thought there was something familiar about him, like I should know him. I was positive I had seen him on TV.

Then I remembered him.

My face went ashen.

CHAPTER 11

"President Charles Sayer?" I gasped. "Is he the president?" He was on a cot, and had a gray blanket pushed to the side. I glanced at Travis for confirmation.

"He sure is. He was out of it when I found him, and I'm not sure what happened to him. He said something about being on Air Force One taking off, and how people started dropping like flies. Then someone forced him into some kind of escape pod or something. He rambled on and on, and made no sense at all, saying his food and water were gone, and he couldn't get out of that pod.

"When I opened the hatch, he said he was President Charles Sayer, and he needed help. I laughed and said I was the pope. He gave me a weird look, saying he had met the pope when he visited the White House, and I wasn't him. I didn't expect that, so I took a good look at him then realized he was the president."

"Wait," Kyle said. "What's he doing here? Last I heard on TV was he was flying back to Washington. He had been in town for a fundraiser when the shit hit the fan."

"The plane didn't make it," I said.

Kyle gave me a curious look. "What do you mean?"

"I saw it go down."

"Where?"

STAND YOUR GROUND

"I was standing in the parking lot at school where your brother left me high and dry."

"Wait a minute, Ella," Tommy protested. He took a step closer to me, invading my space, wanting me to back down. I didn't budge an inch. Not anymore. Tommy's eyes pierced through me, trying to subdue me with silent communication. I intended to stand my ground.

"I told you we needed to get outta there," he said in a loud voice, "but you decided to stay, let me remind you."

"I asked you not to leave me. You ran like a coward!"

"And guess what? I'm alive because of it, and I won't make any excuses for saving myself."

"You're despicable!" I shouted. We were nearly eye to eye, him being only a couple of inches taller than me. My heart was pumping hard, and my adrenaline was coursing through my veins.

Tommy came at me fast, unexpectedly, and using his weight he gripped my shoulders and pushed me hard. Surprised at his aggression, I stumbled backwards and fell on my butt. I wasn't sure which made me madder: The fact he pushed me down, or the fact I was caught off guard. I rocketed up and rushed him, but before I could retaliate, I was yanked back.

"What the hell is wrong with both of you!" Kyle held me by my backpack, forcing me back. "The president of the United States needs help, and you two are arguing over what happened at school? Good God Almighty! Get a grip," he said through clenched teeth.

My breaths were shallow and fast, and it took me a moment to regain my composure. "You're right," I mumbled, flicking my eyes to the president. "Sorry."

"Yeah, me too," Tommy said. "Sorry, Ella."

"Don't ever do that to me again."

"I said I was sorry. My temper got the best of me."

"You need to learn to keep it under control. And let me explain something. If you push, I will push back with everything I have. Everyone here is experiencing extreme stress, and lashing out at those who have helped you is not how to deal with this. We all have a temper. We all have anger, and anger channeled correctly can do great things. What you did was like a two-year old throwing a temper tantrum." I smoothed my shirt down and took a big breath. "Forget it."

I shrugged off Tommy's aggression towards me as a result of everything that had happened. We were all on edge, and wanted to get out of here, and to top it off we had the president, who was injured.

CHRIS PIKE

"Now that everyone has calmed down, and you're past your playground fighting, Kyle, can you help President Sayer?" Travis asked.

"Sure." Kyle set down his bag next to the president and eased onto the cot. "President Sayer? Can you sit up?"

"I think so."

President Sayer pushed himself up by propping an arm on the cot, and when he tried to rise, he couldn't.

"Take my hand," I said. I wrapped my hand around his forearm and he did the same with me, then I pulled him to a sitting position. "Are you okay?"

"A little dizzy." He held his hand to his forehead. "Who are you?"

"I'm Ella Strong."

"Are you my nurse? I don't remember you being on Air Force One."

"I'm not, but I've been trained in first aid. Kyle was a medic in the Navy."

President Sayer saluted Kyle. "Thank you for your service to our country."

"It's been my pleasure, Sir. Now if you don't mind, can I take your vitals?"

Kyle took the president's blood pressure and pulse using a blood pressure cuff Travis gave him. I looked around the engine room trying to find anything useful. To my left was a cabinet, so I opened it. There were various instruction manuals, and a checklist for the train. I rifled through them until I found a book on first aid. Opening it, I perused the table of contents to find a section on concussions, thinking if I had been in that pod, jettisoned to the ground, I probably would have been knocked out. I flipped to the section on concussions, reading it as fast as I could about symptoms and treatment.

"President Sayer, do you mind if I ask you some questions?"

"Not at all."

"Did you lose consciousness when your pod crashed?" I asked.

"I think so." He rubbed his temple with his thumb. "I vaguely recall waking up and being disoriented."

"Okay. Do you have a headache?"

"Only a nagging one. It's mostly gone."

"What about nausea or vomiting?"

"I've been sick to my stomach, but attributed that to the food I've been eating."

"Any blurred vision?"

STAND YOUR GROUND

"It's not too bad now. I'm feeling much better. I think the fresh air has revived me. The air was getting stale in the pod."

"Can you tell me the last thing you remembered before you woke up?"

The president took his time answering, and I could practically see his mind whirling, thinking about what had happened to him, or considering what he was allowed to tell us. I glanced at Kyle, who had finished taking his vitals. He placed the blood pressure cuff on the wall, and disinfected the thermometer. Next, Kyle tested the president's reflexes and examined his neck and head, even looking in his ears.

"Everything looks good," Kyle said. "Blood pressure, temperature, and pulse are all within the normal ranges. There's no bleeding in the ears either."

"That's good news." President Sayer stood, wobbled on unsteady legs, then sat down. "I didn't realize I was so lightheaded. I'm not feeling quite up to par yet." He looked at us for an explanation. "What's wrong with me?"

"I'm not a doctor, but it appears you've had a concussion. A mild one, though. I found a bump on your head, and from the way you answered Ella's questions, a concussion is the only logical diagnosis."

"What's the treatment?"

"Lots of rest, both physically and mentally. You need to let your brain recover, so try to keep the visual stimulation down, such as no TV or video games, not that you play video games, or that the TV is working." Kyle shrugged. "Those are only examples of what not to do. And you have to limit your physical activity."

"That'll be hard to do."

"Why?"

"I've got a country to run, and I need to get back to D.C. I'm still somewhat confused about why it was you and the others who rescued me. Are you my rescue team?"

"I suppose you could call us that," Travis said.

"You don't exactly look like what I was expecting."

"Navy SEALS...guns drawn and everything?"

"You could say that. May I borrow your cell phone?" The president patted down his suit pockets, searching for a cell phone. "I've lost mine. I'm sure the nation is wondering what happened to me."

"Mr. President," Travis moved closer, knelt, and put a hand on the president's knee, "I don't know how to tell you this..."

"Tell me what?"

"There isn't much of a nation left."

"What do you mean?"

"About seven days ago the country sustained some sort of biological warfare attack. The Eastern Seaboard and the Gulf States, as well as northern Mexico and parts of Canada were affected. Many people died. Infrastructure is failing, including cell service. I haven't been able to get a signal in days. We've had ham radio reports of overwhelming death tolls all over the country. It's estimated millions have died."

"It was germ warfare." President Sayer said. "I'm remembering now. I find it unlikely that so many have died. It's impossible."

"No, it isn't, Sir," I said. "An Emergency Alert was issued over the TV this morning."

"Who was it?"

"He didn't identify himself. The man said you were missing, and most of congress was dead. My sister and I witnessed it firsthand, and—"

A scream, primal and guttural and horrifying, sliced through the air and sent shivers up my spine. I immediately recognized who it was.

It was May, and it was obvious something terrible was happening to her.

CHAPTER 12

Central Texas
Fifty Years in the Future

"Ella, are you alright?"

I emerged from a trance. My heart pounded and it took me a long few seconds to get my breathing under control. I was reliving the nightmare of those first few days, and all the memories I had suppressed came at me like a tornado, destroying what was left of my attempts to forget them. Over the years, to keep my sanity, I had surrounded myself with a neon sign blinking loud and clear which indicated *don't get too close to me*. It had worked wonders to keep nosy people at bay, but Teddy had unplugged it, and I was having trouble keeping it together.

"Ella?" Teddy depressed a button on the tape recorder, turning it off. "I'm starting to worry about you. Reliving the first days after the attack is having a huge effect on you. You don't have to continue if you don't want to."

He put a hand on my shoulder, and my tension melted away at the kind gesture.

"Ella, I can come back another time if you'd like me to. This must be hard on you."

I didn't answer because I couldn't. The words were all jumbled in my

STAND YOUR GROUND

head and when I opened my mouth to speak, no sounds came out. It was like a dream I'd had where I tried to desperately scream or warn someone of impending danger, but I couldn't.

I was paralyzed with fear. I had to fight through the helplessness, to push forward, to forget the fear. Fear was in our minds. It was made up, fiction we insert into reality to prevent us from accomplishing what we need to do. I'd overcome fear before. A few spoken words certainly paled in comparison to what I'd been through.

"I guess I should pack up and leave if you're unable to talk anymore. I understand if that's the case," Teddy said.

He reached for his backpack and thumped it on the table. He gathered his pencil and paper, and placed the recorder in his backpack.

I recognized the genuine concern in his voice. He was more concerned about my welfare than recording history. Oddly, he reminded me of Kyle in the way he thought of others before he thought of himself. I had been too hard on Teddy in the beginning, and I realized that now.

My life had come down to an italicized footnote. How bizarre to think the struggles, the absolute horror we endured, would mean nothing unless I stepped out of my comfort zone. I suppose in a hundred years, my story would be forgotten, relegated to a paragraph or a footnote on a term paper, hastily put together so the student could increase the length of the paper in the hopes of impressing the instructor. Maybe the instructor would take an interest in what happened to me by analyzing my story. Perhaps not. Yet my struggle was real, and it happened, as well as the struggle we all faced, and it was up to me to have it documented.

It was up to me to make sure this generation, and future generations, didn't forget. With that resolve I was determined to carry on.

I placed my hand over his to still him. "This is necessary, and it's something I must do. You're the one who needs to hear this." I smiled pleasantly. "I must confess something."

"What's that?" Teddy asked.

"I did a background check on you."

"You did? Why?" Teddy was incredulous at my confession.

"I needed to find out what kind of person you are before I agreed to meet you. I asked our librarian, the one over there," I nodded in her direction, "to send me any articles you had published."

"Really?"

"She did, and quite clandestinely, I have to say. She made inquiries pretending to be a publisher of a new periodical who was looking for a new voice. The university was quite honored one of theirs was on the short list."

"Nobody ever told me," Teddy said.

"That's because we asked for the inquiry to be kept quiet."

"And all this time I thought you had ignored my repeated requests."

"Not at all. I wanted to make sure you were the right person to do this. I've read your works, the honesty involved, the care you've taken with details to get the story right. I must say, you've done superior research. Take, for example, the piece you did about President Sayer."

"What did you think about it?" Teddy pulled his chair out and sat back down again. "I scoured every article and interview I could find about him and what happened when Air Force One went down. He mentioned you."

"I'm aware of that. I read his interview. It's completely accurate except for one part."

"Oh?" Teddy furrowed his brow. "I'm sure I didn't leave anything out. I'm positive I read everything I could about interviews the president made when he was rescued from the pod."

"I believe you when you say you read everything. But there was something important President Sayer didn't mention."

"What was that?"

"He saved the life of a very important person."

Teddy cracked a wry smile. He pulled the tape recorder from his backpack and set it on the table. "Ella, are you ready to continue?"

"I am."

CHAPTER 13

Present Day
West of Houston

The moment May screamed I jumped into action, bolting to the doorway. I put my hands on each side of it, ready to propel myself onto the slippery gravel. My first thought was to leap from the train and burst out onto the land where she had to be. Reason overcame panic because where I stood I had a high vantage point from which to scan the area where I thought the scream came from.

High grass and weeds abutted each side of the incline leading to the tracks, with a line of bushes and trees closer to the highway. Between the grass and the tree line was a patch of thorny dewberry vines. May and I had been reminiscing about picking dewberries. She had to be somewhere near those vines.

The air was still, the sun hot in the sky. I whipped my head from side to side, straining to hear anything indicating where she was. The only sound was the chirping of a bird.

May screamed again, and I pinpointed the likely place. A large oak was about fifty feet in front of me. It was shady and a good spot to take refuge. Standing as tall as I could I saw a flash of blonde hair.

"There she is!" I thrust my arm in the direction of her screams. "She's

STAND YOUR GROUND

by that oak!"

I leapt, and jumped out of the train onto the gravel.

My feet slipped out from under me and I took a hard fall flat on my back, knocking the wind out of me. I gasped for breath, and could neither inhale or exhale, waiting for my paralyzed lungs to work. It took a long second until I caught my breath, and when I did I inhaled as deeply as I could.

In the moment it took for me to be able to catch a breath and to push up to a kneeling position, President Sayer, without regard for his own life or health, catapulted into action.

When I stood, a sharp pain seized my ankle, and I yelped. I took a glance and determined I had sprained my ankle.

Crap.

President Sayer raced past me, jumped over a log, and hurled himself toward May. Kyle and Tommy ran with equal zeal behind him, sprinting like they were jumping over hurdles on a track. They were both athletic, and while I considered myself a good athlete, there was no way I was in their league.

"Travis, stay with the train," I said, not realizing it was an order.

"Good idea," he replied. "I'll keep a look out."

Dusting myself off, I gritted my teeth to prepare myself for the pain when I put weight on my foot. I half ran, half hobbled, skipping down the path laid by the hurried footsteps of the three men. I dashed as fast as my throbbing ankle would let me through the high grass and bushes, branches and leaves slapping my face and tearing at my skin.

President Sayer reached May first, and approached her cautiously, choosing his steps with care as if he was dodging hidden land mines. His eyes flicked around, searching the ground. He motioned for me to stay behind him.

"Here she is!" he yelled. "I found her."

I came to a quick stop right behind him, favoring my sprained ankle.

May's eyes were as big and round as a full moon, and her skin looked like the blood had been drained out of her. She cradled one of her arms and had a bump on her forehead. I resisted the temptation to go to her.

"What's your name?" he asked May.

"Maybelline Strong. May for short. That's my sister next to you. Please don't joke about my name. I'm not in the mood." May's eyes went to President Sayer. "Wait. I've seen you on TV. Are you the…" she gulped, "…the president?"

"I am."

May looked to me for confirmation. I nodded.

"Oh, I didn't mean to sass you."

"That's not important. What's important is what happened to you. Can you tell me what's wrong?"

May sniffled and croaked, "A snake bit me. Am I going to die?"

"No," President Sayer said, using a calm reassuring voice. "Out of all the people who get bit by a snake each year in the United States, only a few succumb to their injuries, and those are usually people with a weakened immune system."

His tone was smooth, and flowed like rich chocolate milk being poured out of a carton into a tall glass. I sure was impressed, listening to him rattle off those facts. No wonder he got elected. If I remembered my facts correctly, he was a fighter pilot, so I suppose those men needed nerves of steel to fly a jet. He was also the epitome of the American dream. He was from the poor side of the tracks, raised by a single mother after the father skipped town upon learning he got a girl pregnant, never to be heard from again until the son he fathered was elected president.

I remember my mom and dad watching the nightly news, amazed that a kid with all the odds stacked against him could rise above his humble beginnings, excel in school, join the Air Force, and become a fighter pilot.

It was his ability to connect with folks of all walks of life that got him elected, my dad said.

"Tell me what happened," President Sayer said. He gently inspected May's arm, turning it over and testing it for flexibility.

"I was picking dewberries when a wasp got tangled in my hair. When I was running around slapping at my hair, I tripped and fell in the vines, and that's when I heard a rattle. I stayed as still as I could, but the snake was right in front of me, and when I put my hand up to protect my face, it bit my arm. I screamed and ran away from it. I bumped my head on the tree, and it knocked me down." She put her hand to her forehead where a red bump had formed.

With a casualness belying the seriousness of the situation, President Sayer said, "It had to have been a rattlesnake. Where did it go?"

She pointed to her left. "I think it went that way."

"You two," he said, pointing to Kyle and Tommy, "spread out and find that damn snake! May, can you stand?"

"Yes."

"Okay. I'll carry you to the train because I don't want you moving

STAND YOUR GROUND

around too much. Be sure to keep your arm at your waist. Try to stay as calm as possible."

President Sayer picked May up as easily as if he was picking up a bag of feathers. He held her in front of him, and she laid her head on his shoulder.

"Ella, you go on up ahead and ask the train conductor if he has a snake bite kit."

Kyle and Tommy came running back right then. Kyle held a headless snake in his hand, the rattle dangling harmlessly. He showed it to May. "Do you think this is the snake?"

She nodded.

"Tommy, you stay here with me. I need you for backup in case anything happens." President Sayer then addressed Kyle and me. "Kyle, you go with Ella, and help her if she needs it. She's hobbling and we don't need another wounded person right now. Each one of us is important, so we need to stay healthy."

I put my arm over Kyle's shoulder, looping it across his back and neck. He held onto my hand and put his other arm at my waist to support me. Together, we made it back before the others did.

When he came to the engine car, Kyle helped me to the first rung of the metal ladder.

"What happened to you?" Travis asked.

"I sprained my ankle."

"Can you make it up?"

"I'll be okay. Give me your hand please."

He extended his hand for me to take it. I grabbed him by his forearm, and he did the same to me. With a firm grip, he hoisted me into the cab.

Still favoring my bad ankle, I asked, "Do you have a snake bite kit?"

Travis scratched his head. "We should have one. I'll check the cabinet where the medical supplies are kept."

Kyle sat next to me. "Ella, you need to lie down and put your ankle above your heart to keep the swelling down."

"I can't. I need to help May."

"You'll be no help to anyone if you make that any worse. You should be good to go by tomorrow if you rest now. Since we don't have any ice, I'll find you some anti-inflammatory over-the-counter medicine that will help. I've got some in my backpack."

Reluctantly, I lay down on the cot and propped my foot up with a pillow. Now that my adrenaline rush had waned, the throbbing in my ankle increased. President Sayer finally reached the cab. He came to the door, and with Tommy and Kyle's help, they hoisted May up. As I was rising from the cot to help May, Kyle appeared and pushed me back down. He handed me two pills and a drink of water.

"Take these and stay there."

He went to May, looped an arm around her waist, and helped her to a chair.

"Hey!" Travis raced back into the cab. "I found a snake bite kit."

"Thanks." Kyle took the kit, opened it, and set out the contents in an orderly fashion on the table next to May. There were bandages, alcohol wipes, a rubber tourniquet, scalpel blade, and a venom extractor pump. I didn't recognize the other items.

Tommy came in, took one look at me, and smirked.

"What's wrong with you?" he asked, smiling the biggest fake smile. "Tired already?"

"Tommy!" Kyle snapped. He catapulted up and stood eye to eye with his brother. "Leave her alone. She sprained her ankle and I told her to lay down."

"Sounds like something you'd say to a girl, right before you fu—"

Kyle's punch knocked Tommy backwards, and he fell to the floor, a thin line of blood drizzled down from his lip. He touched it gingerly, inspecting his mouth for a loose tooth. Finding none, he said, "That's what I thought."

Kyle shook his head in disgust. "You need to leave."

"My pleasure."

Tommy slunk to the door and disappeared, which was typical of him whenever the going got tough. When someone needed help, he was the first to bow out.

Kyle took his time cleaning May's snake bite wound, being careful not to press too hard. When he was done, he put a clean bandage on it and gently smoothed the edges down. Using a pen, he drew a circle around the edge of the swelling.

"May, how are you feeling?"

"It's starting to burn, like someone is putting a match to my skin."

"It's normal for it to burn and sting."

"How long?"

"I'm not sure."

"Aren't you going to try to suck the poison out?" May asked.

"No. It would only irritate your skin and cause the venom to spread

STAND YOUR GROUND

more."

"What about the tourniquet? That should help."

"Recent studies have indicated it's best not to do that," President Sayer said. "It restricts circulation, causing the venom to pool where the bite was. That's bad. The good news is hardly anyone dies of a snake bite. You're young and healthy, so that's on your side. The best thing for you to do right now is to stay calm and quiet. Drink plenty of fluids, and let your body do the rest. I'll check my medical kit in the escape pod. I'm sure there are antibiotics we can start you on."

"Thank you," May said. "President Sayer, I—"

"Call me Charlie."

"Okay, Charlie. You're much nicer than what they've been saying about you on the news."

Charlie laughed, and I admit, even I found that funny. My dad always watched the evening news, requiring us to be quiet and to not interrupt because we would discuss recent events afterwards. It was impossible to avoid the news, and as of this moment I was glad my dad made me watch. How cool was it to meet the president of the United States?

"Well," he said, "don't believe everything you hear on the news."

He stood, and I didn't think anything of it until he stumbled back like he was drunk. He lost his balance and crumpled to the floor.

Kyle rushed to his side. "Ella, what happened?"

I propped myself up on my elbows. "He was helping May, then the next thing I knew he collapsed."

Kyle lifted Charlie's wrist to take his pulse.

"Is he okay?" I asked.

"He fainted. That's all. I'll have to tell him that if he does this again, he could do some damage to himself."

I laughed.

"What's so funny?" Kyle scowled at me.

"It's funny because when you're in the military, you're supposed to take orders from the president. He is the commander in chief. But you're the one giving the orders to him now."

"Well, the president is mortal like we are, and can bleed and get a concussion like the rest of us."

* * *

After the two unexpected events were under control, make that three counting my sprained ankle, Travis gathered all of us into the engine room, and told us it was time we get going.

"Wait," Charlie said. "We can't leave yet."

"Why not?" The irritation in Travis's voice was apparent. "You may be president of the United States, but I'm the conductor of this train, and I say it's time we leave."

"I understand and respect that. Still, we shouldn't leave supplies in the escape pod, especially medical supplies."

"We've wasted enough time, and a few extra supplies won't do us any good."

"It will. We need to take advantage of whatever supplies we have. The pod has more than you think it has."

"I bet it does." Travis raised an inquisitive eyebrow. "There's more than medical supplies in there. I'm not exactly sure what's on Air Force One, but I'd bet my last dollar there's more to this story than you're letting on, and now's the time to come clean about whatever is in the pod you don't want to fall into the wrong hands."

President Charles Sayer cleared his throat. "You're right. Besides a few extra supplies and standard weapons, there is more to the story. What I'm about to tell you is related to National Security. I need your solemn oath you will never discuss what I'm about to tell you with anyone."

The room went quiet. I don't even think Kyle took a breath. Tommy was sitting in the corner sulking, but when 'National Security' was mentioned, he sat up.

"Kyle," the president said, "you were recently discharged, right?"

"Yes, Sir."

"You took the oath of allegiance to the United States when you joined the military."

"I did."

"Then I'm reinstating you."

"My pleasure, Sir." Kyle stood at attention, his eyes fixed on something in the distance.

"Ella, May, Tommy, and Travis. The United States has been attacked, and I need your help right now. I need you to enlist in the armed forces of the United States and to raise your right hand to take the oath of allegiance."

"Excuse me, Sir," May said. "I'm only 16. I'm not sure I'm old enough."

"I'll make an exception in your case, young lady, because we need you.

STAND YOUR GROUND

Are you willing to step up to the plate for your country?"

May hesitated, so I took the chance to intervene. "She's the only family I have left, President Sayer. I'd rather she not enlist. We lost our parents, and I couldn't stand to lose my sister. She's all I have." I pleaded to him with my eyes.

"Ella," he said, "we will all have challenges in the future, difficult decisions to make, and we may not make this out alive, but by God, I'll go down fighting. I will stand my ground against our enemies, and if I die trying, then so be it. This is our home, our land, and I won't stand idly by while some rogue nation comes in and takes what they want. If you're with me, then take a step forward."

The moment was tense, yet I had to act. There was no other alternative. I took a deep breath and stepped forward. May was right by my side, taking her own step. Travis joined us and stood on the other side of me. Only Tommy hesitated.

"You've gotta be kidding me," Tommy griped, his voice filled with anger and frustration. "We barely survived and now you want us to put our lives on the line for what? You?"

"Not me," President Sayer said. "Your country, yourself, and those who survived."

"Tommy," I said loudly to get his attention, "when the going is easy you sure are the big man on campus, strutting around like you own the place. Captain of the baseball team. Homecoming King last fall. It took me a while to see your true colors." My disappointment was apparent as my eyes flicked from his eyes to his feet then back up to his face. "Well?"

"Well, what?"

"Be a man and stand here with us."

Reluctantly, Tommy joined us, standing on the other side of Travis. President Sayer asked us to raise our right hand and to repeat after him. In unison, we began. I said, "I, Cindrella Strong, do solemnly swear that I will support and defend the Constitution of the United States against all enemies, foreign and domestic; that I will bear true faith and allegiance to the same, and that I will obey the orders of the president of the United States and the orders of the officers appointed over me, according to the regulations and the Uniform Code of Military Justice. So help me God."

We took a collective breath, and the mood turned surprisingly jovial. I high-fived May and gave her a hug, followed by another high-five with Travis and Kyle. I lamely slapped Tommy's raised hand in a show of unity.

"Who wants a drink?" Travis asked.
"I do," Kyle said.
"Me too," Tommy chimed in.
Travis gave Tommy a skeptical glance. "You old enough?"
"I am now."
Travis opened a cabinet on the far side of the engine room. Using a screwdriver, he removed two screws, set them aside, then removed a panel. Behind the panel was a bottle of Kentucky bourbon.

Travis cleared his throat. "It's against regulations to have liquor on the train. I only kept this in case of an emergency, and I think this counts as one."

He set the bottle on a flat surface, retrieved several Styrofoam cups, and carefully poured a shot in each cup before handing out the cups to the guys. He offered May and I a drink, but we declined. "You need something. How about a Coke?"

"That'll do," I said.

A moment later, Travis poured May and I a warm splash of Coke.

"I'd like to propose a toast," Travis said, holding up the cup. "To us, our good fortune for being alive, and for finding Charlie, er, I mean the president."

"I'll toast to that," Kyle said.

We all tapped our Styrofoam cups together and took a drink.

"Thank you, everyone," President Sayer said. "Now it's time for us to work together to get that pod on the train."

The room was quiet. I normally would have asked why, but since we were now military, and according to the oath I took, we were to obey the orders of the president.

"Are there any questions?" Charlie asked.

I checked the expressions around me. Everyone was stoic and was either looking at their feet or the walls, or the landscape outside, anywhere except at the President. I decided to speak up.

"I have a question."
"Go on."
"Why do we need to get the pod on the train?"
"We certainly don't want the enemy to get their hands on it."
"What enemy?"
"The people who did this to us, Ella. That's who."

CHAPTER 14

Present Day
West of Houston

Well, that piqued everybody's interest, even May who, as of last week, was more concerned about her outfit matching and the latest gossip at school than matters of National Security. She had been suppressing her tears and masking her pain, and that made me very proud. My little sister, putting on a brave face.

From the concerned expressions, everyone else was waiting on the president to explain exactly what had transpired and what was so important in the pod. I had studied the constitution in class, and learned about world history, but I wasn't versed on the intricacies of foreign affairs. Neither could I grasp why another world power would inflict so much misery and indiscriminate death on innocent people.

President Charles Sayer gathered us around him. The engine room had enough seats for the conductor, the assistant conductor, and the engineer, and fortunately a few more. A plethora of dials and gauges decorated the front panel along with other stuff I had no idea what it was. It looked like a mini cockpit. There were two bunk beds on one wall, which May and I occupied. This was a freight train, not a passenger train, so there were no comforts of the latter.

STAND YOUR GROUND

"Travis was right," President Sayer said. "It's not the water and medical supplies we need. It's the entire pod." He paused to let that sink in. "The escape pod is state-of-the-art technology and design. In layman's terms, it has all the bells and whistles, hula hoops, skipping rope, along with the entire playground. The technology is so new that no other government has it, but I can tell you they know about it, and they want it. The technology is to today what the atom bomb was to WWII, and it will change the face of war. The energy that propels the pod is not a combustible engine, like what a car, an airplane, or even this train uses. It's something different. It's as sci-fi as the warp drive is on the *Starship Enterprise*. The possibilities are endless."

"If you don't mind me asking a question, who discovered it?" Travis asked.

"You won't believe this, but a high school kid from Michigan. One of my National Security advisors saw it on YouTube."

"You gotta be kidding," I said, completely flummoxed.

"I'm not. It was a science fair project. To top it off, he didn't even get an A on the project. You'd be surprised at the crazy things kids come up with, and how the brilliance of their ideas isn't understood or valued. The kid knew, and that's why he put it on YouTube."

"What prevented the kid or his family from selling the idea?" Travis asked.

President Sayer's gaze dropped to the ground. "The entire family was killed in a car accident."

The room went quiet, and we all looked around at each other. Tommy's jaw dropped, and May, being as young as she was, gave me a quizzical look. She was too young to comprehend the president's statement or its implications. Travis crossed his arms, keeping his eyes zeroed in on the president.

Travis finally broke the silence. "Oh? That sure was convenient, don't you think? The U.S. government or perhaps even *you*," he said, "gave the okay to have the family killed? For what? National Security?"

"Look, Travis," President Sayer said, taking a step towards him, "you have to believe me that all I know was the family was killed on a slick road during a thunderstorm. Full stop. The end."

"And I suppose nobody saw the accident," Travis said quite smugly.

"Correct."

"Unbelievable!" Travis shook his head in disbelief. "I always suspected the US government was behind some shady killings."

The tenseness of the room was palpable, and I thought Travis was about to go into bat shit crazy mode. I wasn't sure what his background was, but he wasn't acting like he had just taken an oath to the United States. I had to think quickly, and decided some humor was needed.

"And to think, I was proud of my science fair project I did to determine how long the sun's rays took to burn a hole in different colored construction paper," I commented.

"That sounds interesting," President Sayer said. "How'd you do that?"

"Using a magnifying glass."

"Ella, that's a good project because you can start a fire that way. The sun's rays are channeled and magnified to burn a hole in the paper. It takes longer if it's not sunny, but if it's all you have, it'll work."

He gave me a look like he understood I was trying to divert everyone's attention away from the so-called accident.

"So," President Sayer said, "let's get back on track. If the new technology falls into the hands of the wrong people, the balance of world power will change. That's why we can't leave the pod."

"Okay, wait a minute," Travis said. "So our government knew some other government wanted our new technology?"

"Yes."

"Then why was it being used on the escape pod?"

"Because the previous pod had to have a pilot. This technology is so easy to use, it doesn't need a pilot. The technology can also revolutionize travel. By that I mean cars won't need to use gasoline anymore."

"But you crashed the pod," Travis pointed out.

"Yes, but it's a good thing we had the new pod on Air Force One, otherwise I would have perished. I survived without a pilot, and that's what counts."

"Was anyone left alive on Air Force One?" I asked.

"Only me," President Sayer mumbled. "I was the only one who didn't succumb to the biological agent. All those good people. Gone."

"Talk about draining the swamp," Tommy added cheerfully, pumping his fist.

"Tommy! That's awful." I couldn't believe he said that. "Now isn't the time or place."

"Perhaps, but it's true. Who cares how many politicians are dead? I say good riddance to all of them."

I looked away in disgust.

"Are you old enough to vote?" the president asked.

STAND YOUR GROUND

"I am," Tommy answered in a cocky voice.

"Did you?"

"I don't vote." He put his nose in the air, proud of the fact he hadn't bothered.

"That's what I thought. I've had dealings with people like you. People who are only in this for themselves, who don't give a damn about their fellow Americans. Next time you should consider voting."

Tommy huffed. "You're an old man, and damn lucky to have survived. If it wasn't for us, that pod would've been your coffin."

"Maybe so. But I would have died with the knowledge I've done something with my life. What have you done with yours?"

"I played sports in high school, and I was good enough to get a scholarship."

"Then I defer," President Sayer said with casual indifference. "If you received a scholarship based on grades and sports participation, then that is an accomplishment. Congratulations."

I snorted, and Tommy sent me a wide-eyed stare full of razor sharp daggers.

"Am I missing something?" the president asked, his eyes flicking to me then to Tommy.

"I 'tutored' Tommy in school," I said, making air quotes. "He applied for a scholarship, but hadn't received it as of last week."

"Yeah, Ella, but I was going to get it."

"Now we'll never know, will we?"

Tommy cut his eyes away from me.

"President Sayer, doesn't Air Force One have some sort of protection from biological warfare?" I asked.

"It does, but by the time someone realized what was happening, it was too late."

"Wait a sec," I said. "I was watching TV when I saw a Secret Service man put on a gas mask."

"What? Where?"

"Right before Air Force One was waiting to take off at Ellington Field. It was the biggest news of the morning. The Secret Service men had their weapons drawn, and had formed a barrier to the plane. One of the men put on the gas mask and ran away."

President Sayer had a hard time digesting that. "That can only mean one thing."

"Why? What does it mean?"

"The man knew enough to put on a gas mask before the biological agent hit everyone. He's a traitor. Ella, did you get a good look at him?"

"No. They all looked the same to me. Black suits, dark sunglasses. So you think he knew what was about to happen?"

"Yes."

"Incredible. So what happened? I mean, why did the plane crash? You obviously got on board."

"We didn't get off in time," President Sayer said. "The plane takes in outside air, which gets compressed then funneled to the inside of the plane, meaning the biological agent was sent throughout the cabin."

"Don't you have a filter? Even our house has an air-conditioning filter," I said.

"Good point, Ella. I like that you're not afraid to ask questions. You'd make a good scientist."

"It's possible, but after what's happened…" I dropped my gaze. It was too difficult to talk about.

"You'll be okay," Charlie said. He patted my back then lifted my chin with his hand. "Keep the faith, Ella. And keep a positive attitude. Can you do that?"

"I think so."

"Good. Getting back to what happened on Air Force One, and to your question, the plane does have a filter. I'm guessing the cloud dispersed molecules of the biological agent in front of it. The pilots were worried about the cloud and its effects. Air Force One can't lift off like a helicopter. It takes time to get a jet that size to lift off. So while I was being transported to Ellington Field, the plane had been preparing for takeoff. Doors were shut, engines running, and the moment I ran up the steps to the plane, someone opened the door, threw me in, and shut the door, but not before those molecules in front of the cloud got in. I was rushed to a secure room, buckled in, and we took off without waiting for clearance. That's how the filter system got bypassed."

We all stood there in shock. I couldn't imagine how one simple action of not closing the door in time could cripple Air Force One. It goes to prove every possible emergency was impossible to plan for.

President Sayer continued. "After that, the pilots in the cockpit succumbed first. When they dropped, the backup pilot rushed forward. He dropped dead, then the fourth pilot did, my personal assistant, my National Security advisor, two speechwriters, Marines, a doctor and a nurse, and many members of the press. We were doomed like everybody else."

STAND YOUR GROUND

"That's awful," I said.

"It had to have been worse on the ground." He gave me a sympathetic look.

I nodded. "You must have known something bad was happening because I was watching the morning news that day. I remember reports on TV saying you were being rushed back to Washington."

"I was. We had gotten reports about a suspicious weather phenomenon occurring in the Gulf of Mexico. It's customary for our pilots to be in touch with the National Weather Service to check on weather conditions for takeoff. Specifically, it's their chief meteorologist who alerted us to a strange weather pattern in the gulf. He wasn't sure what it was since it wasn't acting like a hurricane that can be tracked and prepared for. It wasn't a thunderstorm, a tropical storm, or even red Sahara Desert sand that's blanketed Europe before. He told us the cloud was growing bigger by the second, and was expected to reach Ellington Field by 8 a.m. There was no time to waste. Since Houston is only fifty miles from the gulf, it's obvious now the people responsible for the attack knew I was in Houston. They were after me, no matter the amount of collateral damage."

"President Sayer, I have a question," I asked.

"Go on."

"Why didn't they shoot down Air Force One?"

"Impossible. We have sophisticated radar to detect incoming threats. And if by some chance a missile comes our way, we have countermeasures to protect the plane. It had to be done another way. I don't think the enemy counted on Air Force One getting off the ground. I'm positive of it."

"What's next?"

"We can't stay here. The people responsible will be looking for Air Force One, the pod, and me, or what they think is left of me,"

"Why would they want you if you're dead?"

"Because only my DNA will launch the pod."

CHAPTER 15

Central Texas
Fifty Years in the Future

"That certainly was an interesting fact," Teddy said. He clicked off the recorder. "Wow, Ella." He sat back in his chair and clasped his hands behind his head, taking a moment to process all the information I was throwing at him.

"What do you mean, wow?"

"Your memory. It's like this happened yesterday. You've been talking non-stop with such sharp detail. Your story is so fascinating that I haven't even taken notes. I'm completely mesmerized. And I can't believe your memory is so good." He removed his glasses and rubbed the space between his eyes, then placed his glasses back on.

"To tell you the truth, I am too. I haven't thought about that day in a long time. I'm surprised I've remembered so many details."

"This is a history making interview."

"I don't feel like history."

I gazed out the window at the softening hues of the sky, like someone had taken a watercolor brush and swiped it across the heavens. It must be late afternoon, and I briefly thought about the chores I should be doing at the ranch. The chickens needed to be put in the coop for the night, trash

STAND YOUR GROUND

needed burning, the garden needed to be weeded, I needed to check for holes in the wire surrounding the garden so rabbits couldn't dine on my fall vegetables, and buckets needed to be put out to collect rainwater from the storm I suspected would blow in soon. I also needed to make sure the house was secure from intruders, not the human kind, rather the other kind.

I didn't like being outside after dark. The dark frightened me. I couldn't see at night, and my imagination would run wild, thinking the shadows were following my every move.

I needed to get home before dark. I hated the dark, and what lurked in the shadows. I wasn't afraid of humans; I was afraid of the animals who were at home in the dark, using it to their advantage to stalk and attack unsuspecting prey.

Prey like humans, like me.

I shivered.

"Ella? Are you alright?" Teddy asked.

Quickly composing myself, I said, "Yes, why?"

"You're wringing your hands to the point they're red."

"I am?" I glanced at my hands. I wasn't aware I had been squeezing them. "Oh, it's only my arthritis flaring up. If I rub my hands like this," I said, demonstrating like I was giving them a thorough wash, "it helps my arthritis."

"Alright," Teddy said, unconvinced. "You looked like you were in pain."

"I'm fine," I lied. My heart was in my throat.

Teddy removed his glasses, took a soft cloth from his pocket, and cleaned the lenses. He looked at me thoughtfully. "The recorder is off, Ella."

"Your point is…?" I gestured with my hands, inviting him to explain himself.

"I want to know what your thoughts are right now. I want the truth, the kind that's in here," he said, "thumping his heart. Not a filtered memory for the history books."

I didn't answer him immediately. Teddy's a sly one. He pretended to be a clumsy collegiate researcher, hiding behind his glasses and his books. It was clear he understood life. I silently chastised myself, having broken one of my own rules to never underestimate someone by their looks. I'd underestimated Teddy. Earlier, I wasn't sure he was ready for the truth. Perhaps it was me who wasn't ready.

"I have been holding back," I admitted.

"Why?"

"This is hard for me, especially the truth. Do you understand I've done things I'm not proud of; things I wanted to forget? There were things that could eviscerate our bodies with a single swipe."

"Things? Do you mean animals?"

"Yes."

"You don't have to tell me about that right now if you're not ready. Whatever needs to be said will be said in due time. I'm not judging you, Ella. I'm only a spectator in the gladiator battle of your life, watching from the safety of the sidelines."

"It's easier to watch from the sidelines, isn't it? Where you can't get hurt, and if danger does come your way, you have time to react."

"I'd rather be a spectator," Teddy said.

"I'd rather be the gladiator." I lowered my voice. "Fighting to live isn't for the faint of heart. It takes a warrior to live. I was indeed on the battlefield, among the brutality and the violence, my opponents wanting to kill or silence me. Bigger and faster opponents, I'd like to add."

"Yes, but you won in the end, didn't you?"

"That depends on what you mean by won," I countered.

"You get to tell your story, the others don't. That's winning."

"I suppose so."

I glanced down at my hands, wrinkled and gnarled from being in the sun and working the ranch, tilling soil, hammering nails, fixing fences, assisting in the births of calves. Digging graves.

Lifting my head, I checked what Jessica Harbaugh was doing. Her reading glasses had slipped halfway down her nose, perched like a bird on a wire. The chain attached to her glasses dangled on the front of her blouse, and Jessica was fiddling with the chain while she read a book at the front desk. I was jealous of her because I would have liked to have been a librarian, surrounded by people seeking the truth or educating themselves.

Over the years I had developed a sixth sense on when I was being studied or tracked, and I felt Teddy's eyes boring into my soul.

"What are you thinking?" he asked again, his eyes unwavering on mine.

"I'm thinking your books are safe."

"They are. But they are also power. There is power in knowledge, Ella, and I want you to share your knowledge with the world. Every bit of knowledge, regardless of how insignificant you may think it is. I think if you shared it with us, you'd be liberated."

"Liberated?" I scoffed. "From what?"

"From yourself. You've been holding it in too long. What you saw. What you had to do. You're the one who has been hiding, Ella. I'm not the one hiding. We need to know your story. All of it."

"I'd like to forget it."

"But you can't."

"No, damn it, I can't."

"Don't give up now. You're almost there."

"You're pushing too many boundaries," I said, raising my voice. "I don't think I can do this anymore."

Teddy's tensed brow relaxed to one of defeat, and he sat back in his chair, giving me space. I hung my head and massaged my temples, trying to hide my building anger. I supposed he thought he was treading on thin ice with me because I had reluctantly agreed to this interview. I feigned my agreeableness for the noble cause of education and higher learning. I laughed. I was kidding myself, because it was one hell of a story. I was never a quitter, and though this interview was extremely uncomfortable for me, I'd do what I'd always done. March forward.

"Teddy?" My eyes blazed at a thought I had. "If this was a movie, it would have been a great one, containing the necessary elements for a rip-roaring action movie: germ warfare, the United States being attacked, new technology, Air Force One crashing." I paused, lifting an eyebrow. "And a love story mixed in among all that carnage."

"It was Kyle, wasn't it?"

I tossed him a sly smile, dodging his question. "But it wasn't a movie, it was real life." I took a breath. "It was my life, and I kept waiting for the credits to roll at the end and for the lights to come on so I could get back to my normal life attending school, playing basketball, dating boys, getting married one day, and having kids where we all lived happily ever after. My mother did name me after the fairytale princess, Cinderella, after all. How ironic was that, Teddy? That my mother hoped for a fairytale life for me. Instead, my reality was a nightmare."

Teddy placed his hand on my mine. I patted his hand then withdrew my arm. It reminded me of someone I knew.

"Don't pity me, Teddy."

"I'm not. I'm fascinated. Ella, I've read everything I can about you, which I admit isn't much, and I've never come across anything regarding the time right after the disaster."

"I've never spoken about it to anyone. You can only truly understand it if you experienced it. I've read about military veterans being connected through their entire lives due to their combat experiences. They can go decades without seeing each other, but once they reconnect it's like time never happened."

"That didn't happen with the survivors, did it?"

"No. I've also read about survivors of extremely hideous events, drifting apart because the other person experienced what you went through. They know your darkest secrets, some of which are too heinous to revisit. Yes," I nodded, "the survivors have indeed drifted apart. I doubt I'd go to a reunion if there ever was one."

"You wouldn't have to. Most have died," Teddy said. "That's why this interview is so important. To record what happened. I've scoured old houses and places some of the survivors inhabited looking for journals, but there were none to be found. Did you keep one by any chance?" he asked hopefully.

"No. None of us did."

"Why not?"

"Because we didn't have time to write our feelings down on paper, or think of clever sonnets to pen, whiling away the time. We were too busy surviving, trying to find enough to eat, trying to figure out who was an ally or an enemy. The enemies pretended to be our friends, but we found out the hard way that appearances are deceiving. People made alliances."

"I bet you made an alliance with Kyle. Am I right?"

"I guess you could call it that."

"Tell me more."

In one big sigh, I released a life's worth of stress, letting my mind wander back to that time, a time I couldn't imagine what was in store for us. Closing my eyes, the images, the smells, the fear—it all came barreling back to me, and I was transported back to the train where we all were sitting, trying to figure out this new crazy world we had been thrust into.

CHAPTER 16

Present Day
West of Houston

President Sayer had taken a seat in the engine room, and was nursing the drink Travis had poured earlier.

"Instead of using a password, face recognition, or a thumbprint, DNA would be used instead," he told us. "And since each human being has different DNA, except for twins, it would be one of the better safeguards for sensitive data, or in this case an aircraft specifically made to protect the president."

"That's worthy of a movie on the Sci-fi channel," Kyle commented.

"As a matter of fact, that's where we got the idea on the DNA from."

"A movie on the Sci-fi channel? No way! Seriously?"

"I'm kidding." President Sayer grinned. "But they do come up with some wild ideas for movies. *Sharknado* comes to mind." Everyone laughed. "Alright, now that things have lightened up, using my DNA is for real, and it's virtually hacker proof."

"As long as nobody gets their hands on your DNA," I said. "I've watched crime shows. DNA can be found even on a fork."

"That's correct, Ella, but my DNA is protected as much as the White House is. All trash I generate is incinerated in an underground pit, dishes

STAND YOUR GROUND

and utensils are sanitized, and nothing of mine leaves the White House. Even when I'm at a State dinner in another country, anything I use is taken away by the Secret Service."

"Okay, but you still have to start the pod. What do you do, lick it or something?"

President Sayer laughed. "Actually, yes. I lick a plastic card about this big…" He pulled what appeared to be a credit card out of his wallet. "This card works like a credit card when you insert the chip end into a reader. The reader in the pod reads my DNA, matches it to the sequence on file, and if it's a match, the engine starts." President Sayer looked to us for input. "Any questions?"

"Suppose you lose your wallet? Or an operative from another country steals it? Then they'd have your DNA on the card."

"Good point, Ella. Even if that happened, it wouldn't matter. The card is specially made so my DNA is destroyed after one minute."

He was met with a collective mumble.

"Why don't you fly the pod to D.C.?" I asked.

"I would if I could, but the GPS is broken. All I needed to do was to punch in a destination, and voila, the pod would fly there. Since it's broken, it's no use. I could have even used an iPhone to navigate, but those are useless now. Although I could probably navigate the interstates to D.C. by day if I had a map."

"Why don't you?" I asked.

"I forgot to bring a road atlas of the United States," the president deadpanned.

"There's such a thing?" I asked, thinking he was pulling my leg.

"There is. But it's big and bulky, and weighed too much, so decided we wouldn't need it. The pod can only carry a certain amount of weight. In hindsight, we should've had some type of navigation other than a computer driven one. I'll be sure to put in an order for the road atlas. The national budget should be able to handle that expense."

The president winked at me, and I returned a smile, shaking my head at the ridiculousness of a road atlas saving the president.

He clapped his hands once, and said, "Okay, let's figure out how to load the pod on the train."

Kyle said he needed to "detank" which I gathered was man-speak for relieving himself. Tommy followed behind his big brother, probably to do the same.

Travis and Charlie exited the train, and conversed out of earshot. I strained my ears to decipher their hushed voices. A few minutes later, Kyle and Tommy returned and joined Travis and Charlie. They said they needed to break up to inventory what the train had to offer.

There were a few railcars to search, so while the guys checked the train, I decided to get a few winks of shut-eye.

May rested in the top bunk, and I opted for the lower bunk where I could stretch my legs out. If I angled my body from the inside corner to the outside corner, I could dangle my feet off the mattress. These bunks obviously hadn't been designed with taller people in mind. May fit in the bunk like a key in a lock. I worried about her because she intermittently cried from the snakebite, saying it was burning as if someone was holding a red hot coal to her arm. I told her to hang on a few more minutes until it was time for more pain reliever.

She tossed and turned, and I tried to take her mind off her pain by getting her to talk to me.

"What would you like once we get to the farm?"

"Can you heat canned vegetables? And if the fire is hot enough or if the propane is still working can you cook pasta?"

"I will take care of you, May. I'll make sure you eat well and get plenty of rest."

If Uncle Grant was still there he'd probably have fresh venison or turkey for us, and knowing my uncle, he'd probably stocked the cellar with apples, carrots, potatoes, and cabbage. My father and Uncle Grant drilled into us to only keep the vegetables with a shelf life of several months. Each time we made a trip there, my father rotated the produce, keeping to the FIFO accounting method of first in, first out. That way the older produce would be eaten first.

My dad kept meticulous dates on the produce stored in bins on shelves in the cellar. We used to make fun of him, but I'd grown to appreciate the method.

My dad had talked to Uncle Grant before all this happened, telling him we were planning to make a trip there, and possibly live at the farm for at least a year. My dad would never tell me why he wanted to uproot the family from one of the largest cities in the United States to go live on our family homestead located in the rolling hills of Central Texas. I hadn't been too concerned since I would have been attending college in the fall where I'd be in a large city, surrounded by a throng of students. If I wanted takeout pizza, no problem. If I wanted to attend football games, no problem. If I wanted to check out the library, art museums, a lecture on

STAND YOUR GROUND

something other than school, it would have been a ten minute walk from my dorm.

College.

My dreams of college were shattered.

That sure wouldn't happen now, and the reality of our current situation hit me strong and hard, coming at me like a gale force wind. It could have knocked the breath out of me, and it would have, except I decided to fight it with all I had, taking comfort in the fact we were heading to the ranch.

A family trip to the ranch always invigorated me. We couldn't watch TV because there was no TV. Wifi? My dad said no way, which allowed—or forced—May and I (depending on the perspective), to play outside in the shade of the oaks growing in the yard.

It wasn't much of a yard. The grass grew when it rained, and when it didn't the grass went dormant, becoming dry, the brown stalks crunching under our shoes. There were no shrubs to prune or water, and the only flowers were the wild ones which bloomed in the spring, then went to seed, waiting for another spring.

My dad taught me to shoot and to hunt, and to pick the best hiding spots from which to take a shot. Deer were creatures of habit, and took the same trail each day to the best feeding grounds.

I theorized May and I survived because we shared common DNA, so if we survived, then it was possible our uncle survived. After listening to May tossing and turning, the bunk creaking with each movement, I reminded her to keep still and to think pleasant thoughts.

What I most wanted to do was to get to the ranch, away from this city that had taken on the odor of death. Flies swarmed rotting corpses. Some of them had been ravaged by dogs and other animals getting fat off the bloated flesh putrefying under the hot sun. The stench had seeped into my clothes and onto my skin, mixed with my own sweat.

As soon as we got to the ranch, I planned to jump into the spring-fed pool not far from the house. A stream ran along the western border of the ranch where tree branches threaded together forming a canopy.

The water in the spring was a constant seventy-two degrees, and was as clear as a swimming pool, yet without the chorine. In the summer, mottled shade filtered through the leaves, casting shadows on the water. Shimmering minnows darted along the sides, and green water grass swayed in the flow, skipping over the bottom lined with pebbles and larger rocks.

On lazy summer days, when May and I were kids, we would dive to the bottom looking for the diamond necklace my dad said was there. Family lore said a lover, fraught over the death of his betrothed, had cast the necklace into the pool where it would shine for eternity and bring good luck to whoever found it.

Although we didn't believe the story, that didn't keep May and I from searching for the necklace. Perhaps when I got there I'd look for it. We all could use additional luck.

My thoughts took me back to the time when we were kids, and how happy our family had been. A smile crept across my face, and it was the first time I felt safe since the world as I knew it ended. I was exhausted, and I couldn't keep my eyes open any longer. The heat, the loss of my parents, the lack of sleep, May and I injured, our future was…

"Ella? Are you awake?" I opened my eyes a slit to find Kyle kneeling next to me and yawned. I must have dozed off. "I am now. Did you find anything useful?"

"We found a few bottles of water, stale chocolate stashed away in a drawer, two ready-to-eat pasta meals which we decided to split into six equal servings, regardless of who weighs more. That's not what I woke you up for though."

"What then?"

"We need you to sit in the cockpit while we move the pod."

I propped an arm on the mattress and sat up. "You've decided to move the pod?" It was incredulous they'd attempt it.

"We did," Kyle said.

"How?"

"The old-fashioned way."

I gave him a quizzical look. "What do you mean?"

"Elbow grease, and lots of it. When we searched the train for whatever we might need, we found logs in one of the cars, the kind people use to make flower beds with. We will use those and a sturdy rope as a pulley system. We'll roll the pod a few feet then we'll position another log in front of it until we get it on the flatbed. We also found a tarp, so we'll be able to cover it with that."

"What do you need me for then? My ankle is too sore to help push it."

"We need you to sit in the cockpit."

"Get the president to do that. I wouldn't know what to do."

"He says it's easy to work, like driving a car. It'll take all of us guys—me, Travis, Tommy, and Charlie—to push it."

"You're on a first name basis with the President?"

STAND YOUR GROUND

"He did tell us to call him that. We need you to steer it, and Charlie told us the pod is designed to resist movement unless the pilot seat is occupied."

"It sounds hi-tech."

"More than any of us can imagine." Kyle flicked his eyes to the top bunk, then whispered, "Is she awake?"

"Probably not. She's been snoring."

"We thought about asking her to sit in the pilot seat, due to how petite she is, but we didn't want to stress her out more than she already is."

"She's had enough to deal with. Let's let her sleep."

"Can you walk?"

"I can but I don't want to put too much weight on my ankle. Did you by any chance find a crutch in one of the cars?"

"I'll carry you."

"I, uh—"

"What's the matter? Don't you think I'm strong enough?" Kyle stood and playfully did a strong man gesture, showing me his arm muscles.

With an embarrassed smile I giggled and said, "No, no, that's not it at all."

"Then what?"

"Nothing. I don't think it's a good idea for you to try to carry me down the steps from the train."

"I wasn't planning to."

"You weren't?"

"No, Ella." Kyle was the one embarrassed now. He ran a hand over the stubble on his beard. "You can hop to the doorway. Once you're on the ground, I'll carry you piggy back."

"Of course."

"I'd say ladies first, but I need to be out the door before you. Do you mind?"

"Not at all."

Kyle's unexpected chivalry was a welcome surprise, and I momentarily forgot our predicament. I briefly pondered how two brothers could be so different. One who served his country and helped total strangers, versus Tommy, who was only out for himself. In the short time I'd been around Kyle, he had impressed me.

After I hopped awkwardly to the door, Kyle backed up to the steps to make it easier for me to climb on his back. I looped my arms around his neck, careful not to choke him, cinching my legs across his mid-section.

He put his hands under my legs to support me.

"How's that ankle?" Kyle asked as he hitched me up on his back.

"A little sore. I'll be okay in the morning." I had my eyes on an upcoming thicket of vines. "Don't get too close to that."

"I won't. I've been keeping an eye out for more snakes."

"Good to hear."

The sun beat down hot and unrelenting, and I was suddenly aware of my thirst. I glanced at the sky, blue and clear, not a cloud or a hint of one anywhere in sight. It was dry, and I hoped we'd get a rain shower to cool things off.

Kyle carried me to the pod where Charlie, Travis, and Tommy were waiting. Charlie had removed his suit jacket and draped it over a thorny bush. His shirt was stained with sweat and was sticking to his chest. Travis and Tommy were equally sweaty after carrying the lumber from the train to the pod.

"Listen up," Charlie said. "We need to work as a team. Travis, Kyle, and I will take turns ferrying the lumber and pushing the pod. Tommy will push from the rear. Ella will sit in the pilot's seat and steer. Once we get to the flatbed, we'll cover the pod with a tarp, and secure it with rope."

Charlie gave me a crash course on how to steer, then asked if I understood. I told him I did.

"Good," Charlie said. "Let's get this baby moving."

The guys played leapfrog with the lumber and took turns pushing the pod. I sat in the pilot's seat, keeping my hands on the controls, cocooned with only a little bit of room to move around in. Not an inch of space was wasted, yet it was a comfortable space with two padded seats, controls within easy reach, pedals on the floor for acceleration or braking, and though it was a tight space, it was not claustrophobic at all. I even noticed an airplane sized toilet behind a paneled door. A photo of the president's daughter and wife was taped to the dashboard. I squinted at the photo and shaded my eyes from the sun-glint shining through the reinforced glass.

A shadow darkened the sky, and I heard the flapping of wings. Large wings. Not the flapping of a dove...something bigger. I glanced skyward, past the tips of trees and beyond to the empty expanse. A shiver tingled down my spine, a feeling I had a week previous when I heard a guttural sound like a large carnivore claiming a kill.

"Did anybody see that?" I yelled.

"See what?" Kyle yelled back.

"That shadow."

STAND YOUR GROUND

"I didn't see anything." Kyle put down the timber he had been holding then straightened and stretched his back.

"Ella, don't tell me you're afraid of your own shadow or the big bad boogie man," Tommy said, jumping in front of the pod, waving his arms as if he was mocking me.

"It was probably a cloud floating in front of the sun. That's all," Kyle assured me. "Don't pay any attention to Tommy. We are all a little jumpy."

CHAPTER 17

Charlie barked orders and did more than his fair share of the work. That man was no slacker, unlike Tommy, who was pretending to push the pod.

Charlie wasn't afraid to get his hands dirty or sweat like the other guys. Fortunately, they had found several pairs of work gloves in the train, and I'm glad they did because the lumber had enough splinters to tear hands to shreds.

We all worked as a team. I steered while Charlie, Travis, and Kyle relayed lumber from the back of the pod to the front as the pod rolled along. Tommy pushed, although not with much effort. He hadn't even broken a sweat.

Once we reached the train, I hobbled out of the pod and stepped into the engine room, where I sat on a swivel chair. By then May was awake.

"What's going on?" she asked.

"The guys put together a pulley system to haul the pod onto one of the empty flatbeds."

"Do they need any more help? I could probably do something."

"I don't think so, especially considering your snake bite." I reached down and rubbed my throbbing ankle. "They don't need any more help, and besides I wouldn't be much good with this ankle. I think we should stay out of their way."

"Okay." May sounded disappointed she couldn't help.

STAND YOUR GROUND

"But they did ask for you to steer the pod."

"They did?" May's eyes brightened. "Why didn't they come get me?"

I made a sympathetic expression. "May, you were sleeping. I thought it was best you rested. You don't want to mess around with that snake bite. You could make it worse."

"You're right. You're always right, Ella." She had resigned to play the role of the baby in the family, and then she surprised me. "Next time they need my help, I want to pitch in."

"I'll be sure the guys know that."

I was glad to hear her offer to help. I was concerned my little sister's fiery spark had flamed out. She didn't have the in-your-face, youthful bravado prevalent from months past. I supposed there was only so much a person could take. I still had an overwhelming need to protect her since there was nobody else who could. For me, I could protect myself when needed. I was bigger than most girls, I could run fast, and hit where it counted, thanks to a self-defense course I took.

During the time the guys worked to get the pod on the train, I rested my ankle, which had disappeared into a puffy blob of skin and fluid. What I needed to do was to lie down so my foot could be higher than my heart. I searched for anything to raise my foot a few inches. Looking around, I found two books in the console in the engine room and placed them on the bunk I had slept in earlier. I crawled into the bunk and put my foot up on the books.

I rested, listening to the banging and clanging of the guys hoisting lumber, hammering nails and boards in place, and using whatever they could find for a pulley. Some colorful words were used, and frankly it amazed me at the cleverness of using the F bomb as a noun, an adjective, a verb, or an adverb. It made me smile, and for a moment I forgot the seriousness of what they were doing.

Although Tommy was an annoyance, Kyle and Travis were on the up and up, and even President Sayer acted like one of the regular guys. When he rolled up his sleeves, he meant business, and the muscles in his forearms were impressive for a man his age. It was too bad I missed voting in the election by one month; otherwise I would have voted for him.

The minutes turned into half an hour, and before I knew it, an hour had elapsed. I hadn't realized I was so exhausted, and I was so very thankful I didn't have to bear this burden all by myself.

It was unseasonably hot, and the warmth of the engine room lulled me into a fitful sleep.

I woke when the guys piled into the engine room.

"We did it," Charlie announced, wiping the sweat from his brow. "Thanks to Travis's ingenuity, we managed to get the pod into one of the empty flatbeds."

"That's great!" I exclaimed, looking around. Their faces were shiny with sweat. Charlie had his sleeves rolled up, his shirt untucked. Travis had taken off his baseball cap and was fanning himself with it. "Y'all look thirsty. Let me get you a glass of water."

"Ella, you need to keep off your ankle or it will never heal," Kyle cautioned.

"It's fine," I said.

"You may be able to fool some people, but not me. Stay where you are, and let me get everyone a drink."

I reluctantly obliged.

Kyle took three plastic bottles of water, poured them equally into the cups, and handed them out. He put the lids back on the empty bottles, then stashed them in a cabinet.

"Are you keeping the empty bottles for some reason?"

He nodded. "Once we get to where we are going, I'm planning on filling them back up with water."

"Makes sense," I commented. "Where exactly are you going?"

Kyle sat on the floor next to me and crossed his legs, his back resting against the bunk bed. "I'm not sure. I thought I'd go as far as this train went then figure out the rest."

"How far is the train going?"

"Travis said he'd take us about twenty miles west of Waco. After that, he'll check the routes to D.C. so he can take Charlie back there. If there is any government left, he needs to know about it."

"Well…" I trailed off. I was taking a big chance on what I planned to ask.

"Well what?" Kyle gave me a quizzical look.

"You could stay with us at our ranch house. There's enough room. We could ride this out there."

"I don't have anywhere else to go," Kyle said after a moment. "So yeah, sure, why not?"

"I'm coming too," Tommy said, looking straight at his brother. "No way you get to have all the fun with the girls."

Kyle snorted his repugnance at Tommy's comment. "If you consider

STAND YOUR GROUND

backbreaking ranch work fun, then yeah, you'll have the time of your life."

Tommy's face went red. "I was only kidding. Can't you even joke anymore, big brother?"

"That wasn't a joke. It was a backhanded attempt to marginalize Ella and May."

"Alright, alright. Sorry it was interpreted that way," he said, glancing at May and I. Tommy angrily gestured at Kyle then walked away.

"I guess you two don't get along," I said to Kyle.

"Not for a long time. I blame my parents."

"Why?"

"My mother always coddled him and never made him take responsibility for anything. She thought she caused his learning problems by not taking enough vitamins when she was pregnant with him."

"Tommy is very smart," I said. "His problem is that he doesn't want to work hard to find ways to cope with dyslexia. He'd rather play off people's sympathies and—"

"Like yours?" Kyle asked pointedly. "I know about you doing his homework and helping him on tests."

"I thought I owed him because when I was in third grade, all the kids made fun of me. He told one of the bullies if he didn't stop teasing me, he'd beat the kid to a pulp. After that, I wasn't teased anymore. So when we got older I helped him with his homework and tests, and he took me to movies."

"And how did that work for you?"

I folded my arms. This is an inquisition now? He does have issues with dyslexia."

"It doesn't give him a pass for being a jerk."

"Let him cool off," I advised. "Things will get better between you two. A week ago, May and I were at each other's throats. Now we're a team. My dad was right."

"About what?" Kyle asked.

"He said when he and Mom were gone, when our friends had moved on with their lives, that May and I would always have each other. Give your brother time, he'll come around."

"We used to get along, but about the time I left for the service, things changed. I thought it would make him proud, but no. When I came home the first time, he went out of his way to pick fights with me."

"Did you ever ask him why?"

"No. I figured it was a phase he was going through. It doesn't matter. I'm through putting up with his crap. He doesn't have our mom and dad to rescue him anymore."

"I'm sorry to hear about your parents."

"Thanks. You're in the same boat, so all we can do is to move forward and get through this."

Travis and Charlie entered the engine room. Travis went straight to the control panel, and typed on the keyboard. Charlie took a seat on the swivel chair I had been using earlier.

"Is everybody onboard?" Travis asked. "That's only five counting myself. Where's Tommy?"

"I'm here," Tommy said, running up to the engine room. He plopped down in a chair behind the conductor's seat.

"Where have you been?" Travis asked, casting a wary glance at Tommy.

"Checking the cars to make sure we don't have any stowaways."

Travis scowled, unsure if Tommy was telling the truth. "Okay, that's all six of us. Everyone take a seat, and let's get this baby rolling."

The engine room had four seats bolted to the floor like the seats on airplanes, except these were more like first class seats, minus the ability to recline. The leather chairs swiveled, and I found them quite comfortable. To the side were two foldout seats, the kind a flight attendant would sit on when the plane landed.

Travis took a seat in the conductor's chair, and Charlie sat next to him. Kyle and Tommy sat directly behind them. May and I were in the bunk beds.

Since Charlie had been a fighter jet pilot in the Gulf War, Travis gave him a crash course on how to operate the train. "Pretend it's a slow, landlocked jet. The same principles apply, except pretend it's molasses you're pouring while watching grass grow. This baby takes a long time to start, and even longer to stop. If there is an emergency where you must stop quickly, pull this lever," he said. "It's the emergency brake. Although with a train this heavy, by the time you see an obstacle on the track, it's impossible to stop in time."

The windshield was in the shape of a three-sided bay window, allowing the train conductor to have a one-eighty degree view. The instrument panel was covered in different colored knobs and levers, and had multiple computer screens with keyboards.

While Travis worked his magic pushing buttons, keying in commands

STAND YOUR GROUND

on the computer, Charlie divvied up the two boxed pasta meals he had found earlier, and we ate like we hadn't eaten in days. Soon the train sputtered to life, chugging, groaning, like it was an Olympic athlete whose muscles were stiff and needed to warm up before the marathon. The noise the train made was like sitting above the engines on a jet. It was loud, the room was hot, the train rocked, reminding me of sleeping in a boat when my dad and I went night fishing near Galveston.

I imagined I was safe with my dad on a boat somewhere on the bay, listening to the water gently lap the sides, the moon casting a dim glow on the bay. Lights on the shore twinkled like Christmas lights, and muted laughter and music echoed over the water. The stars were overhead, and I'd lay awake searching the heavens for a shooting star to streak across the sky.

Lying here exhausted, my breathing slowed down, my eyelids became heavy, and I could no longer keep them open.

The engine vibrations and noise drowned out my thoughts, and soon glorious sleep blessedly called me where vivid dreams filled my consciousness.

The air was misty, the wind brushed the trees, and colors of the woods segued from morning brightness to late evening shadows, obscuring my vision. I was running through the waist high field of oats in the pasture behind the ranch house. I stopped to look at my dad standing on the porch yelling words I couldn't understand. His words were garbled like he was in an underwater tunnel. He waved his arms for me to return. I laughed and waved back at him, skipping through the wheat, letting my hands weave through the feathery florets.

As I reached the edge of the pasture, dark clouds rolled in, bringing thunder and a sprinkling of rain. A cold gust of wind washed over me, blowing my long brunette hair around. I shivered and goose pimples appeared on my arms. I crossed my arms, rubbing them briskly with my hands, trying to warm myself. Leaves rustled, and my gaze darted to the woods where the shadows grew longer and reached out to me as if warning me of impending danger. A shiver captured me, tingling my spine. I jerked my head around in all directions, thinking I was being watched, though by what, I wasn't sure.

A gunshot rang out, then another zing of a bullet sounded, and I struggled to comprehend what it meant because it was unclear if the gunshot was in my dream.

A voice I did not recognize shouted angry words.

CHRIS PIKE

The pattering of many feet running came closer, and I jerked awake and opened my eyes, my senses on high alert.

CHAPTER 18

I didn't dare move, except for my eyes roaming around the engine room.

I took my time to gather my thoughts about the unfolding situation, wondering if what I dreamed was real or not.

Everything was normal. I mused my dream was the accumulation of years of being forced to watch old black and white westerns my dad loved. Paladin, Josh Randall, the Rifleman, all containing episodes of masked train robbers, jumping off their galloping horses and scaling the roof of the train came to mind. I was surprised I had absorbed enough fictional cowboy mayhem to cause me nightmares.

Calming my rapidly beating heart, I remembered Travis telling us this was a short freight train that didn't transport valuables, except for the Pod, and I didn't think anyone would know about that. The train had several metal boxcars for freight, hopper cars for bulk dry goods, and several tube shaped chemical railcars. Missing were the new model cars being transported and intermodal container cars destined for a seaside port.

Imagining the different cars was like counting sheep. I planned to remember that the next time I couldn't fall asleep. My heart had calmed down, yet the bolt of adrenaline I experienced left me wide awake.

Travis was at the controls, and a freshly brewed pot of coffee got my attention.

STAND YOUR GROUND

Rising, I asked, "Is there enough coffee for another cup?"

"Sure," Travis said. "Help yourself. The caffeine won't do you any good for getting back to sleep though."

"I'm wide awake now." I poured the coffee into a foam cup and took a sip. If I had any hair on my chest, it would stand up. "Wow! This is strong."

Travis smiled. "Said the girl whose last name is Strong."

I laughed. "You can't imagine how people have teased me about my last name."

"Enjoy it now, because when you marry, you won't have it anymore."

Travis was transfixed on the view, squinting into the darkness.

"What are you looking at?" I asked.

"There's a fire in the distance. I've been keeping an eye on it."

"A fire on the tracks?"

"Yeah, and a big one, too."

"A grass fire?"

"No. That wouldn't make flames high enough for me to see it. This is a purposeful fire. One that can damage the rails. I've been slowing the train down, because if we jump the track, we'll be in trouble."

"Someone is trying to stop the train?"

"Yeah," Travis said. "I think we're about to have company, and not the kind you serve coffee to. Ella, do me a favor. Go tell the others to get ready."

"For what?"

"Nothing good. Tell everybody to have their weapons ready." Travis loosened his checkered shirt to let it hang over his belt. I guessed he had a gun hidden under his shirt.

I rushed to the freight car where the president and the others were resting. They were awake and listening to President Sayer, probably hoping they'd hear some White House secrets that would be excellent for party conversations in the future.

"Hey, everybody. Travis thinks we may be facing train robbers, so better get ready for a fight."

Kyle immediately reached into his pack, and President Sayer swung open what appeared to be a clamshell briefcase. It contained equipment secured in place by closed cell foam. There weren't any boxes of ammo, but several transparent amber magazines were filled with rifle type ammunition.

The president looked up at Kyle and I, who were studying the contents of the case. "These are FN P90 submachine guns in 5.7 x 28 caliber," he said. "They are silenced and use fifty round magazines. The ammo is government issue armor piercing since the bad guys tend to use body armor these days. One gun was intended for my Secret Service agent and the other was for me in a dire emergency." He pulled back the ambidextrous cocking handle and let it slam into the battery. "Remember the rounds will penetrate a body." With that warning, President Sayer handed Kyle the first gun and half of the loaded magazines.

The president charged his gun and showed Kyle the peculiar rotating safety selector below the trigger. He put half of his magazines into each of the outer pockets of his suit coat to balance the load. Kyle watched him with increasing interest, which didn't go unnoticed by the president.

"Kyle," he said. "You were more than a medic, weren't you?"

"Yes I was, Sir. I was a Navy corpsman supporting one of the SEAL teams. My dad gave me this 1911 when I came home," Kyle said, checking the pistol to make sure it was in good order. "I'm using Wilson 9 round magazines in this 10mm."

"Interesting. You're quite knowledgeable on your weapons. I had been briefed about the SEAL teams using Navy medics for certain operations."

May had been intently listening to the guys talking. "Can I have a gun? If we are about to be attacked, I need a weapon."

"Can you shoot?" Kyle asked.

"Not very good, but I'm a quick learner."

"May," Kyle said, "the time to learn about guns is before you need to use them. If we gave you one, you might accidentally shoot one of us. The best thing for you to do is to hide behind good cover. We'll take care of everything else."

I was looking directly at May to make sure she understood. She dropped her head. "I guess you're right. I always avoided Dad's offers to go shooting. I never dreamed I would need to shoot anyone. Don't forget I'll be hiding while the bullets are flying."

"We won't. Be sure to stay completely quiet and we'll come get you when it's over." Kyle led May to where a bunch of crates were stacked. "You're little, so get in there and stay low. Can you do that?"

"Yes."

Kyle moved a heavy crate in front of her then whisked away the tracks left in the dust on the floor.

Kyle, President Sayer, and I made our way to the engine compartment. Tommy was nowhere in sight, and I spotted May sneaking out of her

STAND YOUR GROUND

hiding place. I didn't want to make any noise, so I motioned with my hand for her to stay back and out of the way.

Travis had slowed the train to a crawl, and not much distance remained between us and the fire on the tracks.

"What's going on?" President Sayer asked.

"Not sure," Travis said. "I've been trying to assess the damage to the tracks but the flame is too bright. It's blinding me, and ruining my night vision."

"Can you tell us anything about our situation?" Kyle asked.

"The flames are high enough and I'm betting hot enough that the metal rails could have been seriously damaged by warping." Travis shook his head. "It's impossible to see details of the rail. I have a feeling we'll be meeting a large force the minute we step off the train."

"What can we do?" I asked. "We're like sitting ducks. President Say-"

"Call me Charlie. If any of the bad guys hear you calling me the president, I'm dead."

"Okay. We'll all be sure to call you Charlie from now on. Got it everybody? Including you too, May."

"Got it," she said meekly, peeking from behind a chair.

Charlie gathered us around. "In a situation like this, we should be the ones with the surprises. Since they plan on taking over the train, which means the engine room, if we are in here, it'll be like shooting fish in a barrel."

"Why would they want this train?" I asked.

"The pod and me, or what's left of me."

Nobody said a word.

"I'm guessing there was a traitor among my close circle of confidants. Or someone in the Secret Service knows more than they should."

I shook my head. "That's terrible."

"Anyone can be bought for the right price," Charlie said. "Once they secure the train and the pod, they'll repair the track and steal the train. My proposal is to get out of the way until the train is ready to move, then we'll be the hijackers."

"Aren't you worried we might lose control of the pod?" Kyle asked.

"Yes, Kyle, I do want to deliver the pod intact. But we also have a contingency plan." Charlie tapped his wrist. "This bracelet is a transmitter. The pod was set on self-destruct as soon the pod and I were ejected from Air Force One. If I venture more than five hundred yards away from the pod, it will explode with enough force to take out this train. So while we can defend the pod, we also have a backup plan to ensure the bad guys won't get it. I'm willing to take a chance if you are, but the choice is yours."

"You're a smart man, Charlie. It's clear why you are the pres…oops, I didn't mean to say that."

"So what's it going to be? If you want to leave now, it's okay."

"We all took an oath, Charlie," I said. "I'm in."

"Me too," Kyle said.

"Count me in as well." Travis saluted Charlie.

"I'll do my part," May chimed in, stepping forward. "There's one person missing. I haven't seen Tommy in a while."

"Anybody know where he is?" Charlie's question was met with silence. He mumbled an obscenity under his breath and punched his fist into a cabinet.

"I'll go look for him," Kyle offered.

"No, we can't risk you." Charlie put a hand on Kyle's shoulder. "If your brother is lost during this mission, then you can put the blame on me."

Kyle shook his head. "The blame is my brother's, not yours. He made his decision to hide instead of fight. I vote we stick to your plan."

"Okay, then. Let's go."

The group, including May, silently moved to the back of the train then slid out into the surrounding dense brush, some twenty yards away from the tracks. We hid close to the back of the train to avoid running into our attackers by accident. Charlie had said the hijackers' concentration would be on the engine room and the flatbed carrying the pod.

Absolute silence was required while we waited, crouched, hidden among the tall grass and brush. Any unusual noise, like a sneeze or a cough, could alert our attackers to our location.

While we waited, Kyle gave me a silent lesson on how to use the HKS speedloaders for my Ruger .357. He whispered, "When you use up your two fast reloads, use these loose rounds for reloads." I pocketed the extra rounds.

Travis was busy blowing accumulated dust from his WWI vintage 1911. When he finished that, he added a few drops of oil. Later, I learned he had two original spare magazines issued with the gun, evidenced by the half blued finish. He told me his great-grandfather, like so many other WWI veterans, had liberated his issue pistol when he left the Army. This time the government would get back their money's worth since he'd be

STAND YOUR GROUND

helping to protect the president and the prize.

It was obvious Kyle was a gun guy from the start and he had complete confidence in his abilities with the 10mm 1911 he carried under his shirt in front of his right pelvic bone. His FN P90 was less familiar, so he practiced turning the safety switch until it was second nature.

I whispered, "Which one is the best?"

Kyle pointed to the FN P90. "It's quieter, so it will be my primary weapon. But the 1911 is a close second." He put his index finger to his lips, tapped everyone on the shoulder to get their attention. "Shhh. No more talking. They'll be coming soon."

Under the cover of darkness, we waited.

CHAPTER 19

I estimated close to an hour had passed. The glow of the track fire in the distance, visible through the brush, diminished to the point where it was no longer noticeable, leaving only the crackle of heated embers as evidence of its original size.

Voices and footsteps came close to our hiding place. We were lying flat on the ground. I lifted my head only enough to peer through the bushes. Two men were walking the track, using flashlights to search the grounds. One was mid-fifties, the other in his twenties. Each man was armed with an M-4 carbine.

The fiftyish man with salt and pepper hair had on a Hawaiian shirt with large red and white flowers. The younger guy wore an identical print Hawaiian shirt except his had large blue and white flowers. His jeans were dark-washed. I briefly thought the shirt and jeans were odd until I recalled a history lesson learning about militia wearing similar colored clothes to distinguish themselves from civilians. The Hawaiian shirt and dark-washed jeans must be their uniforms. Either that or the guys were in town for a luau. Anyone else could be considered the enemy, therefore could be shot on sight. The man in the red shirt must be the leader.

So this was what battle was like. It was both frightening and exhilarating, and I was determined to do my part.

The younger of the two men said in a perfect American accent, "Sir, are

STAND YOUR GROUND

we sure this is the right train?"

"Our intel is correct. The locator beacon on the pod works like the black box does on an airplane that has crashed. Once we were able to locate the pod, it started moving. We couldn't understand why, until it became obvious it wasn't traveling on its own volition." The higher ranking man swiveled his head, searching the darkness. "The president has to be close by. He wouldn't abandon the pod."

"They must be playing possum, Sir. What are your orders?" His American accent and correct usage of the southern expression was too good to be anything other than American.

"We have waited long enough. I doubt a train conductor or anyone working on this train has the wherewithal to put up much resistance. We need to do a slow and thorough sweep of the two targets."

The commander silently gave directions for his subordinate to search one area, while he did the other.

A minute later, identically dressed men in blue Hawaiian shirts and dark jeans sprinted to the train from four points of entry from the surrounding woods. The first shots echoed into the engineer's compartment. Bullets were fired indiscriminately and errant zings bounced off the metal exterior. We ducked for fear of being hit by ricocheting bullets.

The freight car was filled with the din of two lines of soldiers unleashing automatic hell on everything except the pod. The wooden shipping crates comprising May's hiding place were shot to pieces. I cringed at the thought if she was still there, the floor would have been covered in her blood.

"Pod team clear!" a different American announced, leaning out the car containing the pod. "Pod secure. No damage and no casualties. And no resistance." The American ran his hand over the smooth surface of the pod, admiring it.

Another voice yelled, "Engine team clear! Engine secure and controls operable. No casualties and no bodies."

The man in the red Hawaiian shirt emerged and spoke to his team. "Engine and Pod teams, secure your positions. Where's the pod team sergeant?"

"Here, sir."

"Send four men for track repair."

"On it, sir."

"You," he said, pointing to the engine team leader, "prepare the train for travel to the transfer site. The rest of you find the president! He has to be close by."

We were lying as still as possible when Charlie whispered through clenched teeth, "Get ready."

My heart was beating at breakneck speed, adrenaline flooding my body. My muscles were twitching for whatever I had to do. I glanced at Charlie and the others. May had her head down, while Travis and Kyle had their eyes trained on the militia.

"Attack." Charlie's voice was low, calm, and to the point. The way he held his gun over his head toward the freight car was worthy of a recruitment poster.

We shot up, and sprinted forward like a fire had been lit under our butts.

The side door to the freight car was wide open. The soldiers guarding the pod held their carbines at the ready, yet the sight of the President of the United States running forward with a submachine gun in his hand distracted them.

Charlie and Kyle held the triggers back on their P90s, the suppressors sounding like a cross between a pellet gun and a new muffler. Bodies slammed against walls, fragments of wood and metal splintered into the train car, encased in the bloody flesh of dead men. Travis and I brought up the rear.

The attack was over before Travis or I had to fire our weapons.

We moved forward to check the casualties, making sure nobody was left alive to ambush us.

Charlie offered his assessment. "The problem with quick and dirty attacks is that they are messy. Be careful of the floor. It's slippery. Check for any usable weapons." While I could shoot, I wasn't proficient enough to offer an opinion on whether the guns were useable or not, so while the guys checked weapons, I kept my eyes open for any movement.

The bushes rustled and I spun in that direction, crouching down and bringing my gun up to shoot. It was dark enough to obscure my vision, and time moved in nanosecond increments. I moved my finger close to the trigger, ready to shoot. I wasn't about to let this victory go to waste. Just as the figure emerged, I wasn't sure whether to be ecstatic or—

"May!" The irritation in my voice was apparent.

"What? I heard the shooting stop."

I slapped my hand to my forehead. "I could have shot you!"

"Oh," she said, and glanced around nervously. "Next time I'll be sure

STAND YOUR GROUND

to let you know it's me."

I was so angry, it was all I could do to turn away.

Charlie said, "It looks like only one M-4 is usable. Who wants it?"

"I do," May said. We all looked at her then to Charlie.

Kyle handed May the M-4. "Go back and hide behind the crates that weren't shot up."

"How do I use this?"

"Take the safety off and pull the trigger until whoever is shooting at you is dead."

"Okay," May said, without much confidence.

"Are you strong enough to hold this?"

"I am," she said, demonstrating her hold on the weapon.

"Travis and I will get this baby moving while you guard the prize. If the train isn't moving in five minutes, we won't be either."

Travis and Kyle worked their way towards the engine car. Travis chose the normal entry, while Kyle used a metal ladder to quietly sneak to the top of the railcar.

Travis positioned himself a few yards away from the engine's door, waiting for Kyle to get into position. Kyle used sign language to direct attention to the open side window right behind the main control panel. Once Kyle secured himself on the safety rail, Travis began his run.

He tiptoed up the steps then sidestepped through the doorway. It was difficult for me to see what was happening, but from the yells and confusion, Travis had surprised a group of men. He yelled, "Hands up, everyone!" More shouts resulted, then the sound of Travis's 1911 firing rapidly told the rest of the story as bodies thumped to the floor.

In the miniscule amount of time it took for Travis to shoot the first round, Kyle had anchored his left hand and foot on the safety railing before swinging the right side of his body toward the open engineer's window. His P90's suppressor was less than two feet from the back of a man's head. He jerked the trigger then moved to sight another man.

Simultaneously, Travis and Kyle's expert marksmanship hit the last man standing. He fell to the floor like a brick.

Without wasting any more time, Travis hit the train's throttle, while Kyle made sure no one was running alongside the train, trying to jump on. Satisfied there were no more hitchhikers, Kyle stepped on the catwalk and headed back to the freight car.

My concentration was on Kyle until the cold end of a gun barrel was thrust against my temple.

CHAPTER 20

I had been so focused on Kyle I didn't notice our car had been breached. Out of the corner of my eye, another man dressed in dark jeans and a blue Hawaiian shirt held a gun to Charlie's head. A third man had pulled down one of the remaining crates covering May, and was using it as a chair, like it was his throne and he was a king.

The man holding a gun to my temple pushed it harder, forcing my head at an uncomfortable angle. He removed my .357 Ruger from my hand then relieved Charlie of his P90. The man put both guns on the floor.

I glanced at the seated man who was clearly in charge. He sat there, smug and confident in what was happening. He was the same man I saw earlier in the red Hawaiian shirt. He definitely was the leader, in top shape, and a man who could count on having his men do what he asked. He casually crossed his legs, tapping his foot as if he was bored. "Bring me the president."

One of the men roughly pushed Charlie forward. He stood looking at the man who beckoned him. "So you're behind this? Agent Rick Madden isn't it?"

"You remembered my name. I'm impressed."

"I know all the Secret Service men assigned to me."

"Not well enough, obviously." Madden rose and stepped closer to Charlie, then without provocation, gut punched the president. He grunted and bent over.

Once he recovered from the punch, Charlie straightened. "It wasn't by accident you survived, was it?"

"I don't leave anything for luck. I had a gas mask with me. The others didn't."

"You SOB. Do you know what you've done? The millions of people you've killed? You'll hang for treason."

"I doubt that."

"Who's behind this? The Russians? The Chinese? How'd they get to you?"

"Whatd'ya think?"

"Money?"

"And lots of it," Madden replied.

"You're stark raving mad."

"No, I'm filthy rich." Madden pulled a knife and stuck it to Charlie's throat. "Now tell me how to start the pod."

"I've lost the key."

"I don't believe that for a second. Perhaps if you don't value your life, you might value this pretty little thing." Madden jerked my head back by a handful of hair and put the knife to my throat. He stuck the tip of the blade into my skin, nicking it.

"Wait!" Charlie shouted. "You don't need to do this."

Before anybody could say anything else, Kyle took one step into the freight car and stopped dead in his tracks. His face was sweaty and haggard, and he appeared as if he had used up all his adrenaline.

"If you make a single move, I'll slice her throat wide open," Madden said. "Capisce?"

"Yeah," Kyle said.

"Put your gun in the pile before this pretty thing dies."

As Kyle slowly lowered his P90 to place it on the floor, he used the delay to flip on the safety, unnoticed except for my eyes. I could only think he did that to add a second or two in case one of the militia tried to use it on him. Since he hadn't been searched, I guessed his 1911 was tucked in his waistband. I prayed he wouldn't use it now, otherwise, he'd be a goner.

Madden eyed Kyle's P90 with curiosity, picking it up. "Glad you made the right choice. I admire capable men, so I'll let you off here. Would you like to thank me before you go?" Madden tossed an evil grin to his two subordinates.

CHRIS PIKE

A few tense moments transpired, and I prepared myself for my last moments of my life. Madden was toying with us as a cat would slap around a mouse before killing it. Kyle and I locked gazes. With a subtle movement of my eyes, unnoticeable to anyone except for the person it was meant for, I silently communicated he needed to do whatever was necessary to win this battle. He returned an equally meaningful expression indicating he understood me.

"I would like to say something," Kyle said.

"Be my guest."

"Mayday, Mayday!"

My adrenaline redlined, and as I fought to stay calm, it occurred to me Kyle's coded shout was intended for May, but it failed to elicit any reaction from behind the crates. My heart sank, but I'd be damned if I went down like a coward. It was up to the president and I to do something, anything.

I nodded my head ever so slightly at Kyle, giving him permission to do what he needed to do.

Two of the guards whipped around, looking in all directions, while Madden picked up Kyle's P90. Madden leveled it at Kyle and pulled the trigger. Nothing happened. A confused expression spread over Madden's face until he understood Kyle had flipped on the safety.

In the millisecond it took Madden to comprehend the problem, Kyle jumped out of the car and onto the gravel.

Madden let off a burst from the P90 near where Kyle had rolled out of view.

Madden pulled the emergency stop. "Kill the prisoners!"

Charlie shoved his elbow into his guard. The man grunted, and Charlie struggled to take control of the gun.

With my tormentor's focus on killing Kyle, and the other one struggling with the president, I saw my chance. I reached up and thrust the gun away from my head, turned, and with all my weight I shoved the man holding me toward Charlie.

Bullets whizzed by, and the guards tumbled into each other.

I stretched my body out and dove for my Ruger. Picking it up, I sighted it at my guard, who had his gun now pointed at Charlie's back. There was no time for a perfect shot. I aimed and jerked the trigger hard twice at the man about to execute the president. The shots hit him in the chest, the force of the bullets slamming into him sending the man backwards. He hit the metal wall and crumpled. His eyes rolled into his head and he slumped sideways to the floor.

I swiveled my aim to the man struggling with Charlie.

Tunnel vision took over.

Nothing else mattered. There were no sounds to distract me. My thoughts were clear.

Carefully, I pulled the trigger, and the round blasted a hole in the last guard standing. His body jerked and he was dead before he hit the floor. The reports of a .357 Ruger being fired into what equated to a thick metal can caused my brain to scramble around in my head.

During the moment it took me to gain my wits, Madden made a wild jump out of the train. He landed solidly and took off running.

Kyle rolled out from under the train holding his 1911, jumped up, and sighted it on Madden, but before Kyle could shoot, Madden disappeared on the other side of the train and into the darkness.

As Kyle was about to chase after Madden, I called out, "Don't. Let him go. We need you here."

"No. I need to get him."

"Stay here. I need you to stay with me." Before Kyle answered me, a thought crossed my mind.

May.

She was behind the crates when the bullets went flying.

I rushed to where she was hiding and pushed a crate off her. She was face down on the floor, the M-4 by her side, her hair covering her face. She was so still I was afraid to touch her. I couldn't lose her, and a feeling of revulsion welled in my mid-section. I sat down and put my hand on her shoulder, brushing the hair out of her face. My little sister—

Her eyes popped open.

"May? Are you alright?" Her face was flushed and sweat beaded her brow.

"I think so." She pushed herself up into a sitting position and tucked her hair behind her ears.

"I thought you were dead."

Her gaze went to the rifle. "That's a stupid rifle. It won't work. I tried and tried and kept pulling the trigger to help everybody out, but nothing happened. It's so hot, my arm was killing me where the snake bit me. I guess I fainted."

I laughed. "You missed all the action."

"Oh." She picked up the rifle and held it on her lap. "Why won't this stupid thing work?"

I glanced at the rifle. "Because the safety is on."

"What! I kept pushing it in like Dad told me when he showed me on the .22. I thought they all worked the same."

"You have to flick the safety down to fire the rifle."

"What?" May said, exasperated.

"Thankfully, everybody is okay." I helped her up and we skirted around the crates to join Kyle and Charlie. "You need to learn how to use weapons, otherwise I might shoot you myself."

"You would?"

"No, silly. I'd never do that, but I am going to give you lessons."

"I guess I should've gone with you and Dad when you went shooting."

"That's in the past. It's never too late to learn."

We joined Kyle and Charlie who had moved the bodies of the dead men and placed them against a wall.

"Where's Tommy?" I asked.

"Last time I saw him," Kyle replied, "he was right behind me when we ran out of the brush."

"Hey, everybody!" Tommy hoisted himself into the car. "Wow! Look at all the blood on the floor. Y'all kicked some ass in here."

Kyle moved close to his brother. "Did you see a man running?"

"No."

"He had to have run right past you."

"There wasn't anybody."

"Where were you then?" Kyle's voice was tight with anger.

"I decided to stay in the bushes. Nobody knew I was there."

"What?" Kyle spat.

"If anybody escaped, I planned to take them out."

"You're disgusting," Kyle said.

"What? I had your back and you don't even appreciate it. I thought I was doing you a favor."

Like a bolt of lightning appearing out of dark clouds, Kyle balled his fist and socked his brother in the jaw. Tommy fell flat to the floor.

"What's wrong with you?" Tommy rubbed his chin. "Why'd you do that?"

"Because you're a coward." Kyle stood over his brother, staring him down.

"Why are you giving me so much grief? Travis isn't here. Take out your anger on him."

"He's in the engine room, holding it down himself, making sure

STAND YOUR GROUND

nobody takes it over."

"Oh." Tommy pushed himself up from the floor.

Kyle didn't budge. "Next time, if you don't fight, you're no brother of mine. Understand?"

"Some thanks I get trying to help you out. Believe me. There won't be a next time."

CHAPTER 21

"I can't believe we made it out of there alive," I commented.

Kyle was sitting slumped in one of the chairs in the engine room. I'd taken possession of the chair across the narrow aisle, and May was in the chair beside me, trying to sleep. Tommy and Charlie stood guard, holding weapons, searching for other marauders intent on killing us. I looked upon Kyle with admiration for the bravery he showed, and for the skills and mindset it took him to do what he did.

The train jostled and pitched, rocking side to side. None of us wanted to talk.

"Travis? How much further?" I asked.

"Unless anything else happens, we'll be on the far side of Waco in less than an hour."

I stretched to peer over the dashboard. The bright lights from the train illuminated the tracks, and I followed them until they disappeared into the night. The trees growing on the fence line along one side of the tracks blocked my view. The four-lane highway was visible to the left. Cars and trucks had crashed into one another or had run off the road when the germs from the cloud descended upon their drivers.

A pack of coyotes illuminated by the train's headlights tore at a corpse, and I watched the grisly sight in horrified fascination of the pack mentality. The strongest coyote ate first at the prime cuts, while the

STAND YOUR GROUND

weaker ones darted around, stealing a piece of flesh here and there.

I couldn't get the scene out of my mind.

The train rumbled along the tracks, and the meaning of time slipped out of my control. I thought about my uncle and how'd he react to seeing us. I'd have to tell him about my father and mother not making it.

Uncle Grant had been divorced for a couple of years, and had one son who was a year younger than me. Since his family and mine lived in separate cities, we rarely did anything with his family. I wasn't even sure where my cousin Ethan was, but guessed he was with his mother when the attack happened. In that case, I'd probably never see him again.

"We'll be in Waco in a few minutes," Travis said. "Be ready for anyone trying to highjack the train. Kill them if need be."

The train slowed as we approached Waco, and Travis cut the headlights, letting the glow of scattered streetlights guide him.

The wood frame houses in the neighborhood showed signs of severe neglect. Shutters hung at odd angles. Paint had peeled away, revealing the gray rotting wood. Toys were haphazardly scattered about. A bicycle had been abandoned in a yard. Several cars were on blocks. Whatever civilization had been here before was nowhere in sight. Even chained dogs so common in these types of neighborhoods were missing.

When the Union Pacific train came to the exchange on the west side of downtown Waco, we began a wide loop to the southwest.

"Travis, what are we doing? We need to keep going northwest. Why are we going south?"

"You're quite observant, Ella. While you were sleeping, President Sayer asked me if I could take you as close as possible to your ranch. I said it might be possible since the new line southwest of here connecting UP to BNSF might be open, although I wasn't one hundred percent sure. He wanted to try it. He said it was the least we could do for you and your sister, and the other guys. You all showed incredible bravery back there," he said. "Especially you and Kyle." Travis made eye contact with me. "Ella, take it from me. You're a natural leader, you just don't know it yet."

"I don't want that responsibility."

"It's not yours to want or not to want. People will be looking to you for guidance and sound decisions. Get used to making them."

I glanced at President Sayer, who was oblivious to our conversation. He was intently scanning the countryside.

"What do you plan to do, Travis?"

"Once I drop off you, May, Kyle, and Tommy, I'll keep heading north about thirty miles to where I live so I can check on my wife and daughters. The train passes within half a mile of our house. If they are alive, I'm not sure what I'll do because the president needs me to get him to Washington. I told him I would, and besides, the pod is on the train, and I don't want to be responsible for guarding it. It's just that…"

I waited for Travis to continue. When he didn't, I asked, "What is it?"

"My wife and daughters need me. This was my first opportunity to get out of the rail yard. It was deadlocked so bad I had to manually override the systems. I was lucky to get this train operational."

"Then you should stay with them. I'm sure the president can find someone else to take him to Washington."

"Ella, I'm a man of my word." He looked at me pointedly, troubled.

"Travis, how old are your daughters?"

"Ten and twelve."

"If they survived, then they need you. They may pretend not to, but they do. Every kid needs a dad. You're their father, their protector, so you need to do what all dads should do."

"Ella," Travis said, "you're too wise for your years."

I laughed. "I've been told I'm an old soul."

"I'd say you're a wise soul."

* * *

We didn't talk anymore after that, so I grabbed a few winks of shut-eye I desperately needed. When I woke, we were nearing the sleepy little town of Clifton, Texas, population 3,392 according to the latest census number on the green city sign at the city limits.

It was still dark when Travis slowed the train to a crawl. We approached the downtown area, comprised of only one street lined with tourist shops, a furniture consignment shop, two restaurants, and a bed and breakfast named the Screen Inn. A theater containing two screens sat vacant on the other side of the main highway from the downtown area. A drugstore and a vintage car showroom completed the interest on the main drag.

My plan was to rest at the inn until daybreak, scrounge around for food, then walk or find some means of transportation to the ranch. My ankle had returned to its normal size, so I was pretty sure I could make the walk if needed.

STAND YOUR GROUND

The town was originally named Cliff Town after the limestone cliffs common in the surrounding lands, including our ranch, located about ten miles west of the town. Over the years the city's name was shortened to Clifton.

Our ranch had a notorious limestone cliff with a deep, elongated narrow cave, located high on a rocky hill, dotted with thick cedars and scrubby oaks. It was infamous for being a rattlesnake den where the venomous reptiles hibernated during winter. Tree roots grew into the ceiling of the cave. It was hidden from view by a thick cedar break so dense I'd have to crawl on my hands and knees to penetrate it. At the other side of the cedar break was the prize: the forbidden cave.

My parents were afraid May or I would get bitten by a snake and die if we went by ourselves, so they had forbidden us to go there. They didn't have to worry about May.

It was me they had to worry about.

I never much liked playing by the rules, especially if something was forbidden. Perhaps it had to do with the biblical forbidden fruit. Regardless, I had been told I was a clever girl, so when rules needed to be broken, I made it my business not to get caught.

Though we had been forbidden to hike there by ourselves, I did once, under the guise of hunting for fossils, proof of the inland sea that covered Central Texas during the dinosaur age.

I found out the hard way how slippery limestone was as I hunted for fossils on that steep hill. Even during the middle of the day it was dark and lonely, with only the sound of the wind blowing through the trees. Birds were silent, and even my dad became quiet when we hiked there. He said he was being respectful of the spirits of the people who inhabited the land during the Paleo-American age before the Indians arrived, over ten thousand years ago.

Perhaps when I get to the ranch I'll show Kyle around, and introduce him to the land so he can get his bearings. I'll show him the best hunting grounds, and where the deer bed down during the day.

"Alright," Travis said, interrupting my thoughts. "We're here." He brought the train to a complete stop.

"Ella," Charlie said, tapping me on my shoulder to get my attention. "I would like to say good-bye to you and wish you the best of luck."

"And good luck to you too." I gave him a hug and patted him on the back. "What are your plans?"

Charlie nodded in Travis's direction. "He'll check on his family first.

Make sure they are okay, then we will head on up to Washington."

"Only the two of you?"

"We'll be alright," Charlie said.

"Have you asked Kyle and—"

"You need Kyle and Tommy for added firepower in case the need arises. Besides, I've got a kickass rifle right here, and plenty of ammunition."

"Thank you, Sir."

"Ella, is there anything I can do for you once I'm back in Washington? I'm not sure what I can do, but I'll try."

I thought for a moment. "There is one thing. I loved Cheetos as a kid, but I haven't had any in ages because of my basketball training. If you find a case of Cheetos, I'd appreciate a delivery."

Charlie laughed. "I'm sure I can arrange something along those lines. Does your ranch have an address?"

"I'm not sure of the exact address, but it's easy to find." I pointed at the highway. "Go five miles west from the traffic light. Hang a right at the farm to market road right past the rest stop. Go exactly five more miles, and you'll see the entrance to the ranch."

"What's its name?"

"American Strong. Strong is our family name, and American because that's what we are."

"I like it. American Strong," Charlie said, repeating the name. "It's a great name and easy to remember."

When it came time for Charlie to thank Kyle and Tommy, I stepped back to give him some room. Goodbyes are private and I didn't want to intrude on intimate conversations. I was close to tears myself, so I put my hand to my eyes, wiping them, pretending I had a speck of dust in them. I needed to live up to my last name. Showing emotions right now wouldn't do me any good, and I'd bet my last dollar, Kyle was experiencing conflicting emotions at leaving the president.

Charlie thanked Kyle and Tommy for their help, and released them from the oath they had taken, and when he said his goodbyes to May, he took extra time to comfort her, telling her he had a daughter her age, and if he could ever arrange it, he'd like them to meet. When he said his daughter was a cheerleader too, May's eyes sparkled. Apparently, cheerleaders had the same type of camaraderie as other athletes. I guess May and I were more alike than I wanted to admit.

I hopped down to the ground, heaved my backpack up on my shoulder,

STAND YOUR GROUND

then stepped away from the train, as did Kyle, Tommy, and May. I nodded to Travis, who was in the engine room at the controls. Charlie was on the catwalk.

"Good luck to you!" I yelled as the train chugged forward.

"And to you too!" Charlie yelled over the churning and squeaking of the train.

Then they were gone, the early morning darkness swallowing them, the train's lights fading away until it was like it had never been here. I hoped they'd make it, and I hoped Travis would find his family alive. If not...I don't even want to think about it.

In the darkness, my gaze went to the twinkling stars in the heavens. The quarter moon glowed low in the sky, beckoning me to keep my eyes on it. Closing my eyes, I prayed silently to keep Travis and Charlie safe on their travels. When I opened my eyes, I could have sworn the moon winked at me as if to tell me my prayers had been answered.

May had recovered enough from her snake bite and was able to walk on her own, although I carried her backpack.

"Ella, let me carry that," Kyle said. "You've got enough to carry."

"I won't fight you on it." I handed May's backpack to Kyle.

Tommy had walked on ahead, reminding me of when he left me high and dry in the school parking lot. This time I didn't plan on running after him or asking him to stop. Besides, it was plain rude for a man to walk in front of a woman, unless it was a safety issue, and I doubt Tommy was looking out for anyone's safety other than his own.

"Let's find out if the Screen Door Inn is empty," I said. "If so, I want to rest there until daybreak."

"Aren't you afraid of the boogie man?" Tommy asked. "Oh, that's right, you are!" He laughed.

"There's a difference between being scared and being cautious. I'm being cautious. If you want to go ahead of us, then go. I won't stop you. You heard the way to the ranch. Be my guest, go ahead of us."

Puckering his lips, Tommy blew out, "Oooh. Bossy now, are you?"

I ignored his taunting. Whatever game he was playing, I wasn't going to participate by acknowledging him.

In the middle of town, the four of us silently crossed the highway which divided the town in half. Streetlights were dark, and it was impossible to see through the glass plate windows of stores, and the only movement was a cat scurrying around a corner building. I had expected corpses to litter the area, and I found it odd there were none.

A strange odor wafted on a silent breeze, and I spied a smoldering heap of charred indistinguishable forms and tree stumps with tree limbs sticking out. On a second glance those were no tree limbs. Those were arms and legs. It appeared someone had made an effort to clear the town of the bloated corpses, which meant there were possible survivors. Their location was the big question.

I was ready to start the long hike to the ranch, but traveling at night wasn't a good idea. My ankle was still tender, and I wasn't about to take a chance of reinjuring it.

When we came to the inn, I was about to open the front door when Kyle stopped me.

"Ella, you and May stay back. I'll clear the hotel. When I tell you it's safe to come in, then you can."

"I'm coming with you," I said.

"No, you're not trained like I am."

"Maybe not, but I can still shoot."

"Okay, tell you what." Kyle ran a hand over the stubble on his chin. "You and Tommy stand guard at the door. Deal?"

"Deal," I said.

"What about me?" May asked.

Kyle thought before answering. "Check the four cars parked in front here," he said, motioning to the SUVs and one sedan. If any are open, search for anything useful. If you find something you can carry, then take it."

"Like what?"

"Weapons, food, a map."

"I can do that," May said.

"Once you're done," I said, "May and I will find a room to share. If you're tired, you're welcome to stay with us."

"You two go on and rest. After I'm sure the place is okay, I'll check the kitchen for anything useful."

"Good idea. I can help you."

"It's not necessary. I'm fine, but if you find any men's clothes that aren't blood stained, I'll be much obliged."

Kyle tentatively opened the door. It squeaked, and in the quiet of the night, it sounded particularly loud. He froze. I crouched and whipped my head left and right, looking for movement, for I was sure the sound was so loud it could have wakened anyone.

A few tense seconds ticked by. "All good," I whispered. "Nobody's out

STAND YOUR GROUND

there."

Kyle closed the door, leaving Tommy and I to stand guard. May went from car to car, checking if the doors were open. If it was locked, she gave me the thumbs down, indicating she couldn't open it. All she needed was a brick or a crowbar to break the window, yet we had not reached the point where it was okay to destroy property.

When she reached the fourth car, she popped her head up and gave me the thumbs up sign. I mouthed *good job*.

I returned to keeping my eyes on the far parking lot, searching for any movement.

A high pitched scream made the hair on my arms stand up. Then a low growl and snapping of jaws together jolted me into action.

May!

CHAPTER 22

I sprang up from my crouched position and bolted to where she was. My .357 was in my hands, and I was ready to shoot. I dodged a tree growing in a circular patch of dirt in the sidewalk, then looped around a car.

When I approached May, she was wide-eyed and had her back against a car opposite the one Kyle told her to search. She pointed at it.

Cautiously, I stepped toward the car with the back windows rolled down half way. My gun was raised, my heart thumping.

I stepped closer, but in the low light, it was difficult to discern much of anything. "Shhh!" I whispered to May.

I removed my backpack, unzipped a compartment, and removed a flashlight. I flicked it on and shined it in the car to find a large dog huddled in the backseat, trembling and panting. It was brown and black with golden tufts of hair above its amber eyes. Its hair was bristly, and appeared to have a smattering of German shepherd, along with other indistinguishable breeds. A leash was still attached to its collar, and the tags jingled when the dog moved. Then it occurred to me the dog had been in the car for over a week. I found it incredible it had survived a week without food or water.

"We can't leave it there," I said.

"What should we do?" May asked. "Let it go?"

STAND YOUR GROUND

"I'll give it water first."

I retrieved the silicone expandable bowl from my backpack, which in hindsight I was glad I packed at the last moment. I shook it open and poured bottled water in it. I approached the car and spoke in soothing tones to the dog. It cocked its head, listening to me. Reaching in, I unlocked the car then cautiously opened the door. The smell from the dog having relieved itself in the car was overpowering. I grimaced and breathed through my mouth. The dog eyed me warily, and without making eye contact, I continued to talk, telling him everything would be okay, and that he was safe. Without making any fast movements, I set the bowl of water on the seat then closed the door, but not all the way. The dog greedily lapped the water until it was all gone.

After the dog had his fill of water, it wasn't as nervous as before. I cracked open the door and, taking a chance, I extended my hand so the dog could sniff it. I inched my hand closer until my fingers were near its muzzle. I kept my hand in the dog's line of sight so I wouldn't spook him. Hesitantly, the dog ran its black nose over my fingers then surprisingly, he licked my hand.

I moved my hand to the collar, and held his tag up. Squinting to read the small print, I said, "Your name's Ruger." I gave him a quizzical look. "Ruger, huh?" The dog cocked his head. I turned over the tag to read the other side. "You're vaccinated too, that's good," I said, as if the dog understood me. The address of the vet clinic where the dog had been vaccinated was in a city, miles away. I pondered why his owners were here.

"What's his name?" May asked.

"Ruger." My expression turned sad. "I think his owners were on vacation here."

"Oh."

"I'm betting they were either in that pile of burning bodies or they were guests at the inn since their car is parked here."

"Why would they leave their dog in the car?"

I shrugged. "Who knows? They might have been checking in and getting their room ready when this all went down. At least they cracked the windows open for the dog."

Kyle strolled up to us. "Whatd'ya find, Ella?"

"A dog."

"Is it alive?"

"Yeah, and *Ruger* is hungry and thirsty."

Kyle scratched the side of his face. "Ruger you say?"

"Uh huh."

"I have an idea." Kyle opened the driver's door, popped the trunk, and skirted around me to peer inside it. "Exactly what I thought. Dog food and guns. If only his name was M-4." Kyle cracked a wry grin.

May laughed. "Gun humor."

"I'm beginning to like Ruger's owners." Kyle nodded approvingly.

"Why?" I asked.

"You won't believe what's in here," he said excitedly, his voice rising. "There's a Ruger GP100, and a Ruger Redhawk in 10 mm. These just came out. It's the same caliber as my 1911." Kyle lowered the trunk lid. "Do you think Ruger's owners would mind if I borrow these?"

"We saved their dog. I think they'd be okay with you borrowing their guns," I said making quote signs with my fingers when I said the word 'borrow'. "You'll return them, right?"

"Of course I will." Kyle scowled playfully at me. "Now all I need is a cold beer, a pickup truck, and my life will be complete."

"You forgot something."

"What?" he asked.

"A girl in tight jeans," I said, waggling my eyebrows.

He moved closer to me. "Are you the girl in tight jeans?"

"I might be."

"Do you want to be?" Kyle asked, moving closer to me.

I was afraid to answer.

Kyle moved close to me and whispered, "Maybe I'll take you out on a country night sometime. The two of us, under the moon and the stars."

I grinned at our playful banter.

Kyle pocketed the guns and the ammo. "May, would you mind holding the dog food?"

"Not at all."

Kyle rummaged around in the truck for anything else that might be useful. I tried coaxing Ruger out of the backseat by gently tugging on his leash, but he wouldn't budge. I stepped back and cooed his name in the sweetest voice I could muster. "Ruger, come on boy. Come on out." He only stared at me. I tugged some more, unwilling to yank him out, deciding that wouldn't be the right thing to do.

"Ella, try this," May said, handing me a handful of dog food.

"Great idea." May poured a few pieces of kibble in my hand, and when I offered the food to Ruger, he gobbled it down. She handed me more, and instead of reaching in to Ruger, I kept my hand away from him. He inched closer to take the food. I repeated the offering of food until he was at the edge of the seat. Finally, I coaxed him out.

"The inn is clear," Kyle said. "I put an X on one of the rooms because there are two corpses in there."

"Man and woman?" I asked.

"Yeah," Kyle replied. "Why?"

"You'll see."

I gently coaxed Ruger away from the car and to the inn. Potted plants were positioned on each side of the blue front door, trimmed in a muted green. The reflection of an American flag in the window and the first rays of the morning sun caught my attention, and when I saw my reflection, I was horrified. My hair was a mess, my face red, and dark circles were under my eyes. I swear a streak of gray at my temple had appeared overnight. I supposed after what all I had witnessed, it was to be expected. In a matter of days I had become older than my eighteen years. I shrugged it off, trying to be positive because I had survived while others hadn't.

Stepping into the lobby, Ruger was skittish at first as his eyes roamed over the enclosed space. The lobby was light and airy, with carefully placed lamps and various books and magazines.

Two lightly colored striped wingback chairs complimented the dark sofa placed strategically so guests had their backs to a wall. The wood floors creaked as I stepped over to the front desk. I spied a basket of peppermints, and since my sweet tooth needed satiating, I pocketed a handful of the mints.

"May, come with me. I need your help."

"Okay," she said. "But I need to rest before we start the long hike to the ranch. If we find an empty room, I'll take a nap."

"I'm not keen on a long walk either," I replied. "Hopefully we won't have to."

"Ella," Kyle said. "Don't go in Room 4 that has an X on the door. It's a grisly scene. If you want to, you can leave Ruger with me. I'll keep an eye on him."

"He's coming with me," I replied. "There's a reason."

"Alright." Kyle yawned, took a seat on the sofa, then stretched out. "I'll catch a few winks here." He turned to Tommy who was loafing by the front door. "Lock it. I don't want any surprises."

The front door lock engaged with a thump, so if there were any unwanted visitors, not that we had seen any people, they'd have to kick in the door or break the windows to get in. I felt safer knowing that, but wouldn't feel completely safe until I got to the ranch.

When Kyle's head hit the decorative sofa pillow, he was out. I went over to the front desk, opened a cabinet behind it to find the master keys to the rooms, and took the one marked Room 4.

May and I crept up the stairs, Ruger followed obediently beside me, navigating the stairs with ease. At the top of the landing, I glanced down the hallway. On the door to Room 4, an X had been scrawled in big letters. I led Ruger to the door and eased off the leash, letting it dangle loosely.

Ruger lowered his head and sniffed the space at the bottom of the door. He ran his nose the length of the door, taking in the odors. The odor of the dead bodies was so strong I had to swallow the bile rising in my throat. I placed my hand over my nose, thinking my dirty hand smelled better. Ruger whimpered several times then pawed at the door.

"Ella, what's he doing?" May asked.

"His owners are in there."

"How are you so sure?"

"Ruger recognizes their smell."

"Ohh. That's awful." May turned away in disgust.

"Hold Ruger, please. I'm going in."

"What for?" A horrified expression washed over her face.

"I'm going to search for car keys. Since Ruger's owners are in there it means the keys to their car are in there too. The roads are clear here, so all we need is a car to get us to the ranch. I needed Ruger to identify his owners. Even dead, I figured he'd still be able to identify them. That's why I needed him. I don't want to search any more dead bodies than I have to. Hold Ruger back. Don't let him in the room."

I retrieved the room key from my pocket. Right as I was about to open the door, May said, "Ella, take this." She handed me a scarf. "Put it over your nose. You'll need it."

I held it to my nose and steeled myself for the scene on the other side. I opened the door, squeezed in, then shut it behind me.

The odor in the room was so overpowering my eyes watered. Two bloated bodies were on the bed. The man had his arm over the woman as if trying to protect her. Their skin was mottled purple blue-black in places and bodily fluids had leaked out of orifices, staining the cream colored coverlet.

It was all I could do not to vomit, knowing I would have to search the man's pockets for the keys.

STAND YOUR GROUND

As I stepped closer, I glanced away from the gruesome sight. As luck would have it, I spied a purse on the credenza, next to the TV. It was an expensive purse, tan leather, the kind under lock and key in department stores. I snatched the purse off the credenza, turned it upside down, and dumped out the contents on the floor. Various makeup compacts scattered around, lipstick, a cell phone, a wallet, a hairbrush which I pocketed, lip balm I also stuffed in my pocket, credit cards, a checkbook, receipts, and a pamphlet showcasing a local animal sanctuary where tigers, wolves, cape buffalo, a giraffe, and a honey badger called home. I scattered the contents in a wide circle, searching for keys. I didn't find any.

The keys had to be here, and I sure didn't want to dig around in the man's pockets. I glanced at the purse again and noticed the side compartment was snapped shut. I opened it, and bingo.

I now have keys.

No exhausting long hike necessary or wasting time searching for other keys. I was ready to get to the ranch and if it meant sitting in dog pee, so be it.

Right as I was about to dash out the room, I remembered Kyle needed a clean shirt. I quickly rummaged through the closet, found several shirts, and tugged them off the hangers. I dashed out the room and shut the door. "May!" I said with excitement in my voice. "We have keys. There's no need to stay here. We can drive to the ranch and be there in a few minutes and sleep in our own bed. Come on, time's wasting."

I tugged for Ruger to go, but he wouldn't budge an inch. Though he was half starving and dehydrated, he still had a lot of strength in him. The water and food must have invigorated him.

"Come, Ruger," I said, giving the leash a gentle tug. The dog wouldn't budge. I tugged again, and he twisted and shook, trying to wiggle out of his leash.

"Ella, he doesn't want to leave his owners in there," May suggested. "You'll have to let him say goodbye."

I was horrified at the thought of going back in there.

"Open the door and let him go in, Ella."

She was right. Dogs were smarter than we gave them credit for. I opened the door and led Ruger in. He glanced at me, as if he needed my approval. I petted him on the top of his head then down between the eyes. I dropped the leash, and said, "Go on. You need to say goodbye."

Ruger took several cautious steps towards the bed, stepping around the scattered contents of the purse, his tail tucked between his legs. He lifted his snout, sniffing the mixture of life and death wafting in the room, and when he came to the bed, he put his nose to the cold gray hand dangling over the side of the bed, sniffing the curled fingers.

Ruger sniffed some more, then rested his snout on his owner's hand. He stayed like that for a few moments until I picked up the leash and gave it a tug. He didn't resist this time, and when I guided him to the door, he stopped, took one last look at his owners. I reluctantly shut the door on the only life he had known.

His owners obviously had taken care of him and loved him, and it showed in the way he treated their bodies. We all had suffered loss, and now I had one more life to be responsible for, although I didn't mind because having a dog comforted me, especially since our family dog had died six months prior.

It was time to go, and our footsteps were heavy with sadness. May and I padded down the stairs, Ruger following us.

When we came to the bend in the staircase, Tommy and Kyle were sacked out on the sofa, dead to the world.

"Wake up," I said, jostling Kyle. "I've got keys to a car."

He yawned and cracked open an eye. "Hmm? What's going on?"

"I've got keys to the car we rescued Ruger from."

"You do?"

"I do. Ruger alerted me the dead people in room 4 were his owners."

"You went in there?"

"Uh huh. And I found these keys." I tossed them up then snapped my fingers around them for emphasis. "These will save us a long hike."

Kyle propped himself with an arm. "The dog communicated that to you? How?"

"I'll tell you later. Get your things and let's go. I'm ready to get to the ranch."

CHAPTER 23

"Oh, man, does this car stink!" Tommy exclaimed.

Tommy was sitting in the back seat with May, Kyle was in the passenger seat. Ruger sat between Tommy and May, who was stroking the nervous, panting dog. I was driving, and had only traveled a mile when Tommy started complaining.

"Next time I'll be sure to stop by the car wash to get it detailed to your liking." I glanced over my shoulder and threw Tommy a world class smirk.

"I don't like sitting in dog pee," Tommy huffed.

"I'd be happy to stop the car so you can walk the rest of the way. It's a genuine offer too."

After a few moments of silence, he asked, "How much further?"

"Less than ten minutes. I'll take a right at the rest stop, then once we're on the dirt road, it'll be no time at all."

We were all tired and dirty, and the first thing I planned to do was to go to the spring and take a bath.

Near the house, my ancestors had built a windmill for pumping water, which was collected in a cistern. We needed to conserve as much water as possible, considering the long, hot summer was nearing. Days of blistering one hundred degree temperatures were the norm in July and August.

My grandpa told us when he had to work the ranch, he and his brother

STAND YOUR GROUND

would start working at 6 a.m. By 10 a.m. they had to stop because it got too hot for the horses. They'd eat a meal, sleep the afternoon away, eat again, then they'd start working around 7 p.m. They carried lanterns with them so they could work until midnight. With all that hard labor, no wonder they were lean. In the black and white photos of that time, the women were older than their years and had shriveled like a prune by the time they were forty, laboring along with the men in the hot sun.

Turning the car into the entrance of the ranch, I announced, "We're here. The house is about a hundred yards down this road."

"I hope Uncle Grant is okay," May said.

"He has to be," I replied, because if he wasn't, I wasn't sure what to do. We'd have to make it on our own.

I pulled the car to the gate and stopped. Before I could open the door, Kyle said, "I'll open the gate. What's the combo to the lock?"

"1600," I replied.

"As in 1600 Pennsylvania Avenue?"

I smiled and nodded. "It was Uncle Grant's idea."

"I'm beginning to like your uncle."

"If Uncle Grant is here, then it shouldn't be locked."

Kyle tested the chain, and called out, "It's not locked. It only looked that way."

I pulled the car through and Kyle shut the gate.

The unpaved rocky road curved to the topography of the land. Scrubby live oak trees lined the sides, and at times the brush was so thick it obscured the line of vision to the creek running parallel to the ranch boundary. A few hardy wildflowers were still blooming, and bees flitted from flower to flower.

Century old trees lined the creek, and that was where the treehouse my dad built me was. It was like a little one room house, with a carpeted floor, two windows to take advantage of a cross breeze, a shelf containing books, and the kitchen—if it could be called that—had a place to prepare food. A foldout table and two chairs rounded it out. The last time I was there, my dad had stacked a case of bottled water for emergencies, along with a first aid kit, and ointments for bug bites. There was no running water, although a pulley system had been rigged to haul up larger items when necessary. Two bunk beds lined one wall, and I hoped a mouse hadn't taken up residence in the mattresses. I'd find out as soon as I said hello to Uncle Grant.

The treehouse was anchored to a huge oak tree, and used two of its sturdiest limbs as a supporting beam. To gain entrance to the treehouse, my dad installed a ladder, which could be hoisted up like a drawbridge in case Indians attacked, my dad explained playfully. The switch to lower it was placed on a nearby tree, hidden in a natural hole. My dad said it was to keep trespassers out; another switch was located inside the front door.

I drove another fifty yards, the white caliche dust billowing behind the car, blanketing the oak trees in a gray haze. A good rain would wash it away.

Finally, the old homestead house came into view. The two-story house had been built in the 1800s when my ancestors settled on the land. Long windows placed strategically in the rooms allowed for cross breezes to cool the house in the summer. In the winter, several fireplaces heated the house. We never had central heat or air in the house, even when it became available. I suppose that was a good thing now, considering there was no more electricity.

When the heat of the summer became too much, I'd slip down the steep stairs leading to the cellar so I could cool off. The door to the cellar resembled a closet door, and could be bolted from the inside. My ancestors made it that way in case of Indian attacks, not that there were any when they finally made it to Central Texas, but they were told to construct the cellar for safety and food storage.

There was also a narrow tunnel leading from the cellar to the side of a hill about a hundred yards away. My parents warned May and I never to crawl into the tunnel, citing the unstable beams. At this point I wasn't even sure if it was passable.

I cut the engine to the car and put it in park, then honked the horn twice to get Uncle Grant's attention.

His truck was parked in front of the house so he must be close by.

"Let's unload and go on in," I said.

"Where should we put our stuff?" Kyle asked.

"There's one bedroom downstairs, three upstairs," I said. "May and I will take the one with two single beds. You and Tommy can have separate bedrooms, whichever ones Uncle Grant isn't in."

Kyle slung his backpack across his back then hoisted May's on his shoulder to help her out because she was still feeling the effects of the snake bite.

I let Ruger out of the car. He lifted his snout, his nostrils twitching and working, taking in the smells of the land. His eyes took in his new surroundings, and when he looked toward the creek where the trees are

STAND YOUR GROUND

thick and the ground damp with leaves, he growled low in his throat.

I patted him, smoothing down the ruff standing up on his back. "It's okay, Ruger. Nothing's there, other than an armadillo or some wild hogs."

Ruger looked at me, whining, those dark eyes, trying to tell me something. "What is it, boy? What are you trying to tell me?"

Tommy sidled up to the house and as he was opening the door, I said, "I wouldn't go in. Uncle Grant doesn't know who you are. He's been known to shoot intruders before."

"No way," Tommy said, snorting a huff.

"If we had internet, I'd Google his name so you could read the article about a house invasion. The thugs picked the wrong house. Grant's house to be specific. He was a former policeman who went into the security business, so I wouldn't mess with him if I was you. He especially doesn't like smart asses, and he's always armed. Plus, he's got a mean dog who doesn't like strangers."

That did the trick. Tommy backed away from the front door.

Leading Ruger to the house, I coaxed him to walk on the pathway of stones collected at a local creek. Smooth, pancake sized stones, washed and tumbled clean by water and other elements. As kids, May and I would always take time to turn over the stones, looking for a prized horned toad.

Before entering, I rapped my knuckles on the door and shouted, "Uncle Grant! It's Ella. Are you here? I'm here with May and a couple of other friends." I waited for an answer then tried again. No luck, so I turned the doorknob, and to my surprise it was locked.

"What's the matter?" May asked.

"The door's locked. We never lock the door."

"That's kinda stupid," Tommy commented. "You should always lock the door."

"It doesn't matter out here. If someone wanted to break in, a locked door wouldn't stop them. It's better to keep it unlocked so there's less damage if they do. When nobody's here, we keep the main gate locked."

"That's his truck, right?" Kyle asked.

"It is," I confirmed.

"Then he can't be too far away. Maybe he's walking the fence line or something. Or out in the pasture."

"Possibly, but it still doesn't explain why the door is locked."

"Didn't Mom and Dad used to keep a key under one of these rocks?" May asked.

"Yes. It should be under the seventh one from the house." Walking along, I individually counted the rocks, and when I came to the seventh one, I turned it over. Spying the key, I said, "You're right, May. Here it is." I held it up for everyone to see.

When I entered the house, I immediately shivered, not the kind from the cold, but the kind from an ingrained sixth sense, announcing loud and clear to be careful.

I stood with my mouth agape, trying to comprehend the scene. It was absolute chaos. Chairs were turned over. Lamps lay askew on the floor. Magazines were scattered everywhere. Cushions on the sofa were halfway on like somebody had used it as a lever to propel themselves for a jump. Broken dishes were scattered on the floor in the kitchen. Two windows were broken.

"Do you think this was a break in?" I picked up a lamp and righted it, then bent over to pick up two bottles of whiskey next to the sofa. "I guess Uncle Grant and J.D. had a party all to themselves."

"Who's J.D.?" May asked.

"Jack Daniels."

"Oh, I get it. Bourbon. Hand those to me," May said. "I'll toss them in the trash."

"This was no burglary," Kyle said.

"How do you know?"

"Because drawers haven't been opened." Kyle went over to the broken window to inspect it. "That's odd." He peered outside the window then looked at the ground. "The window was broken from the inside. Glass shards are below it. But on this one, the break-in was from the outside."

"Let me get this straight," I said. "Someone jumped through a window to get in, then jumped out another one to leave?"

"It appears that way."

"There must be another explanation. I'll check the house to see if Uncle Grant is sleeping. May, you stay here with Kyle and Tommy."

"I'm coming with you." Kyle stepped closer to me.

"It's not necessary."

He lowered his voice and looked at me pointedly. "That wasn't a request. I'm coming with you."

"Alright." I was glad Kyle had stepped up to the plate. Something bad had happened here, and I needed backup. After finding my mom dead, I wasn't sure if I could handle finding another relative dead.

"Tommy, stay here with May. Ella and I will check the house."

"Now I'm a babysitter?" Tommy huffed and plopped down on a chair.

STAND YOUR GROUND

May had already taken a seat on the sofa.

"Deal with it," Kyle shot back without missing a beat.

Once we were out of earshot, I asked Kyle, "Is he always like that?"

"I'm afraid so. He's felt entitled all his life." Kyle opened a closet door and pushed clothes and boxes around. Satisfied it was clear, we headed down the hallway. "I think it was because he was the youngest, and my parents let him do anything he wanted to."

"I've never seen that side of him until now. Oh, wait a minute. I have." I stopped and put my arm on Kyle. "Last week at school when everybody started dropping like flies, Tommy and I were in the same class. I told him we needed to stay and get help for these people. He told me I could stay, but he was leaving. I begged him to stay, but he left me. He sure did play me."

"Get used to it. He knows he can't do that to me, which is why we clash all the time. I don't take his crap anymore. When he was little I had to, otherwise my parents would punish me. But once he got as tall as me, my gloves came off. Hey," Kyle said, "let's talk about this later. We need to check the house for your uncle."

"You're right. Family dynamics can wait."

"Stay behind me please, Ella. I need to check this bedroom."

Kyle had his 1911 in front of him, both hands on the pistol. He bobbed his head around the door, took a quick peek, then dashed in and crouched. He looked under the bed, checked the closet, and behind the curtains.

"It's all clear," he said. "How many bedrooms did you say you have?"

"Three more upstairs."

Kyle and I crept up the stairs, trying to make as little noise as possible. The stairs creaked with each step. In the quiet of the house, each step was magnified, and I was sure if anyone else was here, they'd hear us approaching. Once we were on the landing, I motioned to the bedrooms. Kyle checked each one, and finding nothing, he went to the next. I was on the lookout in case he had overlooked anything.

Kyle came out of the last bedroom. "He's not in the house, but he has been. His stuff is in the bedroom. Any ideas where he might be? Does he have any friends around here? A secret hiding place?"

I thought a second before answering. "The cellar. We didn't check the cellar."

"Where is it?" Kyle asked.

"We passed right by it. The door is to the right of the stairs."

We filed down the stairs so fast our steps sounded like the clatter of hooves on pavement. As Kyle reached for the doorknob, a blast shattered through the door, splintering wood at us.

I jumped.

Another zing of a bullet whizzed by us.

Stunned, I could only think to drop to the floor and cover my head. Kyle crouched and took cover.

Tommy and May rushed into the hallway.

"What's going on?" Tommy asked.

"Get down!" Kyle shouted. "Someone is shooting at us!"

Tommy forced May to the floor.

"Who's there?" Kyle shouted.

We waited for a response.

"Get the hell outta my house! I don't know who you are, but if you don't leave by the count of three, I'm comin' out and blasting your sorry hide into the next county. I'm not bluffin'! One, two—"

"Uncle Grant? Is that you?" I shouted. There was no answer. "It's me, Ella, and May is here too. I've got two of my friends with me. Don't shoot, okay?"

We waited for a response. A few agonizingly long seconds ticked by. I shot a glance at May. I mouthed, "That was Uncle Grant, right?"

She nodded. "And as cranky as ever."

Then the door to the cellar opened, and my uncle stepped out. Kyle had his gun aimed, ready to shoot. Tommy and May had managed to slide out of the hallway and into the den. I took one look at my uncle and I knew something was terribly wrong.

CHAPTER 24

Uncle Grant emerged from the cellar, his hair disheveled, a few days of beard growth on his face, and his eyes were big and red, the whites of his eyes flashing like those of a mad man. I wasn't even sure if he recognized me.

"Uncle Grant, it's me, Ella, your niece, and that's May," I said, pointing to her. "What's wrong?"

His gaze bounced all around the room as if he was searching for something.

"Lower your gun, please," I said. "No one wants to hurt you." I took a tentative step towards him, and gently guided him away from the cellar door, thinking if he wasn't careful, he'd fall down the stairs.

When Kyle placed his hands on Uncle Grant's rifle, Uncle Grant said, "Over my dead body, you will."

Kyle backed off. "Whatever you say."

"Let's go sit in the den," I suggested.

"Okay," Uncle Grant replied.

"May, find him something to drink," I said. "Water, juice, a soda."

"Skip it. Get me the bottle of bourbon from the pantry." Uncle Grant's voice was raspy. "And don't bother with a glass."

"On it," May said.

We took Uncle Grant to the den, and had him sit on the sofa. I sat next

STAND YOUR GROUND

to him. "What happened in here?"

He didn't answer immediately, instead he went to one of the windows, peering outside. "What day is it?"

"Friday."

May handed him the bottle. He unscrewed the cap and took a long pull, swallowed, and wiped his mouth with the back of his hand. "I needed that."

I exchanged worried glances with May. Our uncle had never been like this. "Uncle Grant, how long were you in the cellar?"

"A day or two. I lost track of time. Could have been three."

"What happened in here?"

Ignoring my question, he took another swig of the whiskey. "Damn, that's good stuff. Any of you boys want some?"

"Don't mind if I do," Kyle replied. Rising off a chair, he approached Uncle Grant and offered him a handshake. "I'm Kyle Collins. That's my brother Tommy."

"You got a good, strong, handshake. I like that. Are you two friends of my nieces?"

"Uncle Grant," I butted in, "Tommy and I went to high school together. Kyle and Tommy are brothers. So yes, we are friends."

"Good enough for me."

"Grant, can I call you Grant?" Kyle eyed him.

"Sure." Uncle Grant handed Kyle the bottle then went back over to the window.

Kyle took a swallow of the whiskey, eyed the bottle, reading the label. "Kentucky bourbon. The best."

"Next time I'll be sure I've stashed a bottle in the cellar. That's one thing your daddy forgot to do, Ella."

"Grant," Kyle asked, "are you searching for something out there?"

"I'm not sure."

"Did it have to do with what happened in here?"

Uncle Grant was searching the land, looking beyond the pasture and to the trees lining the creek. "My mind is playing tricks on me."

"How, Uncle Grant?" I asked. "Tell us what happened. This wasn't a burglary, was it?"

"I wish it had been." He sat down, obviously troubled by what he had experienced. "Ella, I, uh…I can't explain what I saw." I joined him and put my hand on his shoulder. "It's okay. We're here now."

Ruger came up to Uncle Grant and nosed his knee. "Is that your dog?"

"He is. His name is Ruger. We found him trapped in a car in town. He was thirsty and hungry, but okay."

"Keep him near you. Animals have a sixth sense. He can protect you."

"Where's your dog?"

Uncle Grant hung his head. "Taken."

"Taken? Taken by who?"

"Who isn't the question, Ella. It's *what* took him."

"What do you mean?"

"I can't talk about it now." Kyle gave Uncle Grant the whiskey bottle. He took another swig. "God, I need this. Calms the nerves."

"You do whatever you need to do." I shot a worried glance at Kyle. "If you don't want to talk about it, you don't have to."

"I'd rather not. I'm not even sure if what I saw was real or not."

We made small talk after that disclosure, discussing the weather, the crops, Kyle's military service, my basketball scholarship, May's cheerleading. We took turns relating our trip here, the train incident, the president, the pod, and most importantly what was for dinner. Uncle Grant said he had a few venison steaks that had probably thawed by now in the freezer, but were still good. He told us the electricity had shut off the day before he locked himself in the cellar. I told him about what my dad and I saw on TV the day we were attacked. I hated to tell him my parents were dead, especially his brother.

"Ella, if anyone could have survived, it would have been your dad," Uncle Grant said. "Why did I live and he didn't?"

"I can't answer that, but I'm so glad you made it."

"We're family, all of us, including you boys," he said. "Family watches each other's backs."

"That sounds like something Dad would say."

"It's something your grandpa told us when we were little."

"Well, Uncle Grant," I said, standing. "I'm going to unpack what we have, get settled, and take a bath."

"We have well water, but please only use what you need. The dry season will start soon, and we need to conserve as much as possible. The water will be cold, but better than nothing."

"Thanks for the heads up on that."

* * *

The afternoon went by quicker than I had expected, each of us doing

STAND YOUR GROUND

chores by setting up the house for five people, inventorying supplies, and I had been so busy I forgot to take a bath. May was sleeping, and Uncle Grant, Kyle, and Tommy were having some much-needed male bonding time by the outdoors grill. My dad had splurged a couple of years ago by having a covered outside eating area built. It was constructed from rock, and had most of the bells and whistles of a modern kitchen, including five chairs and a table.

Many memories had been made sitting around that table.

I let them enjoy the moment, laughing, telling stories, having a beer. Slipping out of the house unnoticed, I snatched a bar of soap, a towel on my way out, secured my revolver, and left through the side door.

I needed to hurry. It would be dark soon, and I didn't want to be out here by myself after the sun dipped below the horizon.

I navigated the sloping hill dotted with trees, patches of cactus, and tall weeds until I came to the spring. A willow tree offered graceful shade, its branches heavy with green foliage, hung like Christmas tree lights.

I took my shoes off and dipped my toe into the chilly water to test it. Although it was colder than I recalled, I quickly acclimated to the temperature. I removed my clothes and placed them on a low hanging tree branch, keeping the towel within reaching distance. Since I had not told anyone where I was going, my concern about being found with only my birthday suit on didn't worry me.

Soft grass tickled my toes, and dappled sunlight streaming through tree branches danced on my shoulders, warming them.

It was quiet except for the cooing of a mourning dove.

I stepped into the clear spring-fed pool, took a breath, and submerged, my toes stretching to the bottom lined with pebbles and moss. Opening my eyes, I watched a school of minnows darting to the shallows, weaving around larger rocks, searching for a place to hide in the soundless universe.

For a few precious seconds I blocked out the world above, which helped me rejuvenate. I surfaced, took a breath, and pushed my hair out of my face. After a quick look around, satisfied I was still alone, I submerged again. I splashed in the water, and when my lungs needed oxygen, I sucked a quick breath then submerged, letting the water wash away the worries of the world, clearing my mind of its troubles. I reached to the bottom and pushed around pebbles, searching for the diamond necklace May and I used to look for.

Somewhere hidden among the shiny pebbles of chert the necklace must be there. I spotted lavender colored chert, lime green, mocha, sea foam green, baby blue with white dots looked like a robin's egg. Others were translucent clear pebbles, so many washed smooth by eons of tumbling. I dug my hands into them, letting them filter through my fingers like sand.

As I let the last handful of pebbles slip away, a shiny string, glinting in the last rays of the sun, looped around my fingers. I stared at it a moment, wondering what it was.

Then it hit me.

The necklace!

The necklace with a solitary diamond the distraught lover had tossed into the pool, the one May and I had searched for, was in my hands.

I shot to the surface, clutching it.

I needed to tell somebody. I could hardly contain my excitement.

Emerging from the pool, I looped the necklace around my neck and secured the clasp. I couldn't wait to show May.

Looking around, I hadn't realized how quickly dusk would be upon the land once the sun dipped below the horizon. A few minutes earlier it was still light, and now it would be dark soon. Something rustled the leaves in the bushes along the creek, and the melodic birdsong of the woodlands stopped suddenly, turning into sharp notes screeching like a needle raked across a record.

The woods where I had played, where I took comfort in, instantly transformed from a place of solace to a scary place. Trees grew darker, the shadows longer. I had been afraid of the dark since I was a kid, imagining all sorts of crazy stuff that wasn't real, like monsters hiding under my bed. Right now my imagination was running like an out of control locomotive.

The entire time I had been at the pool, I had been listening to the chirping of a bright red male cardinal, twittering musical notes of coupling, trying to lure a female. Then the melody was disrupted in mid-tune, cut off into a long shriek.

A red fox ran blindly through the underbrush right towards me, unfazed by a human, its eyes wide with panic.

Another fox bolted behind it, completely disregarding me.

I quickly stepped out of the pool and without towel drying, threw on my clothes, checked my revolver, and—

A force so powerful, so unexpected, crashed into me, knocking me back into the water. My revolver flew out of my hand and I hit the water with a huge splash, sinking a foot below the surface.

Instinctively I closed my mouth and eyes.

STAND YOUR GROUND

My first thought was that Tommy had played a trick on me by sneaking up unnoticed. It made me angry and I couldn't wait to tell him off.

I opened my eyes underwater to a swirling trail of crimson caught in the flow of the slow current. I rationalized the sun was shining off an object, and projecting its color into the water.

Rocketing up to the surface, I was ready to unleash the full fury of my wrath on Tommy. It would be the last time he ever scared me. I pushed my hair away from my face.

"Tommy, you—"

CHAPTER 25

I was too shocked to finish my sentence, and the hair on my neck stood on end.

What was it? I'd never seen an animal like that. It resembled a wolf, but what wolf has fangs as long as a knife? Its fur was gray along its back, the sides black. It was larger than the stuffed wolves displayed at sporting goods stores where children gawked at their magnificence. Comparing it to a Clydesdale horse would do justice to its size, but horses weren't built to kill.

The beast circled me and lifted its snout, sniffing. Its paws were the size of a dinner plate, with retracting claws like a cat's.

My heart was thumping fast, and I was becoming lightheaded.

The beast paced along the shore, keeping its eyes on me. The breath it snorted was hot and rank with the stink of death.

My breathing was labored, my leg heavy and clumsy. Stars appeared in my vision, twinkling, and the sky darkened. I fought to stay conscious, because if I lost consciousness in the pool, I'd drown.

I started to black out and was unable to hold myself upright. The trees around me swayed, and the sunlight dancing on the leaves drifted away, withdrawing its light. I was dizzy and teetering in the water. I sank down, letting the water cover me to my shoulders, then to my mouth. I was so tired my head felt like it weighed a hundred pounds. Strangely, being in

STAND YOUR GROUND

the water comforted me, like I was hidden and protected, a watery sheath that couldn't be breached.

Someone was calling my name in the distance, garbled, like the person had a mouth filled with marbles.

"Ella? Ella? Are you here?"

Water sloshed around me, and I was chilled to the bone. I couldn't distinguish who was calling me or from what direction. It was like being underwater where the sounds are a garbled mishmash of the universe, languages of foreign words with no meaning.

I opened my eyes to blurry images matching the distant garbled words. "Ella. Ella! Where are you?"

My hands floated in front of me and I flexed them, staring at them like they were the most fascinating things in the world. The fingertips were shriveled like a prune, ridged and lined, so clear, yet so blurry.

A bubble left my mouth and I followed its track upwards.

I *was* underwater.

I didn't want to die. Not yet, not now.

I kicked to propel myself above the water line where I gasped a deep breath.

Tommy was walking towards me.

He stopped in mid-stride. "There you are." His tone was scolding. "We've been looking all over for you."

I continued to stare at him as he came closer to me. "What are you doing in there with your clothes on? Everybody is worried about you. Aren't you going to say anything? And why the heck is your pistol way over there?"

I looked at him quizzically as he reached for me, offering me his hand, telling me to take it. Using what little strength I had, I muttered, "Get away. Get out of here. Run for your life."

An expression of disbelief spread across his face. "What did you say?"

"Run..." I coughed out.

"Ella, what's wrong?" His gaze went to the water. "Good God. You're hurt. There's blood all in the water. Give me your hand. I've got to get you back to the house."

"Nooo." I was having a difficult time forming words. My brain was clouded with thoughts and images. *The necklace... so cold...the beast.* I gasped a breath. *Kyle. May. My parents...*

Tommy jerked his head around, startled by a low growl coming from the woods. "Who's there? Is that you, Kyle? If it is, that's not funny." He paused. "Stop joking around, I mean it." He looked at me then back to the woods. "Ella, stay there. Don't move. There's something moving in the woods."

The beast that knocked me into the water emerged from the thick woods and zeroed in on Tommy. With claws extended, its massive legs claimed the ground, and it opened its mouth, revealing long fangs meant for slashing.

A horrified expression washed over Tommy's face. "Ella, don't move," he said without moving his lips. "I'm going to try to distract it so you can run." He fumbled for his pistol. His hands were shaking so much he couldn't remove it from the holster. He slowly backed up to put distance between himself and the beast.

"The treehouse!" I screamed. "Run to the treehouse!"

When he turned to run, the beast sprang up and leapt effortlessly, covering twenty feet in one glide. It pounced on Tommy, knocking him to the ground, pinning him with those massive paws. Tommy feebly reached around, clawing, reaching for its eyes.

I stumbled deeper into the water.

As if to toy with Tommy, the beast slapped him around, playing with him. When Tommy finally unholstered his pistol and brought it up, getting off a wild shot, the beast sliced off his arm with one swipe of its paw.

I flinched at the brutality.

Tommy's pistol, still clenched in his severed hand, tumbled away, leaving a trail of blood. There was no way he or I could get to it. I needed a weapon. Where was my revolver? I scanned the ground, but it was nowhere in sight. What could I use? A stick, a rock? I found none, so I yelled and waved my arms to distract the animal.

Blood spurted out of what was left of Tommy's arm, and he looked at it, puzzled. I don't think his mind comprehended what had happened. He wiggled out from under the animal, crawled a few feet, then the beast pounced on him, smashing him into the ground.

Tommy was quickly tiring.

Then, as if the beast was tiring of the game, it released Tommy, letting him stumble a few more feet.

I yelled, "Ruuun!"

The beast gave me a look that sent a chill through me, as if telling me I was next. It sensed I was wounded.

It turned its attention to Tommy, and in one impressive movement, it reared its head back, opened its mouth, and slammed into Tommy's neck,

STAND YOUR GROUND

crunching through bone and knocking him to the ground.

Tommy's entire body jerked once, and his right foot twitched spasmodically for a few seconds, then he moved no more. The beast put a paw on his prize then slowly licked Tommy's bloodied stump and his neck where blood spurted out of the wounds.

I screamed loud and shrill, and the beast lifted its eyes at me, blinked once, as uninterested in me now as if I was a rock, a tree limb, nothing.

Rising off Tommy's body, the beast thrust its head to the sky, opened its mouth, and roared to claim its kill. The fierceness of the sound echoed through my body and blasted into my head, chilling me more than the cold water encasing me.

The beast tore at Tommy's corpse, tearing through flesh and fabric, blood oozing from its mouth and dripping to the ground.

I watched the beast dig its fangs into the limp corpse, stand, and trot away, carrying Tommy's body like a lion would a freshly killed gazelle.

Was this happening? Was that really Tommy? I must be hallucinating.

I blinked my eyes and squinted through the low light.

I slapped my face to wake myself.

All I could think was that I needed to survive.

I shivered uncontrollably, and if I didn't get out of the water, I'd die, and that thing, that animal would tear my body apart.

Mustering what little strength I had, I crawled out and onto land. I lay there exhausted, my face mashed into the grass, willing myself to move. I pushed myself up and took an unsteady step, then another and another, dragging my leg like a fifty-pound weight was tethered to it.

I picked up Tommy's arm and pried his fingers away from the pistol. If the beast came back for me I would be able to protect myself.

I fell or maybe I didn't, I don't know, as I walked like a drunkard to the treehouse ten yards away. It might as well have been one hundred miles. It felt like a marathon.

Placing one foot in front of the other, I stumbled to the ladder, and mustering strength from deep within, I hoisted myself rung by rung to the safety of the treehouse, where I collapsed on the porch.

Getting an idea, I thought I could shoot a round to alert someone to my location. I swept the porch with my hands searching for Tommy's pistol. Finding it, I fired several shots.

It was no use calling for help; my voice was too weak.

I rested on the hard boards for a few seconds, breathing hard and trying to get enough oxygen, and it was then my leg started throbbing from my thigh to my calf.

Although I was shivering uncontrollably, my leg was warm in places. I was too afraid to look at it so I concentrated on getting through the door.

I dragged myself in using my arms, then kicked the door shut, safe for the moment.

Lying there shivering in wet clothes, my mind was a muddle of discombobulated thoughts and images, recalling snippets of conversations and people who had come and gone in my life. I laughed at one point, and cried another. I was fatigued, more exhausted than I could have ever thought was possible. My eyelids were heavy and I fought to stay conscious, forcing myself to focus on the ceiling made from untreated wood. The pattern fascinated me, and I counted the smoothed ridges from one board to the next.

One, two, five, eight. I counted each line.

Three, seven…

I'm so tired.

I jerked awake from my own snoring.

Bored with the ceiling, I hummed a tune, or didn't. I'm not sure.

I closed my eyes again, unable to fight blessed death and its temptation to be relieved of this pain. My parents waited for me, there in the expansive sky, in the heavens where the moon and the stars shined and twinkled their magic. I was ready to be reunited with them. I no longer cared about my body or who would find me or when, and I drifted into unconsciousness to a place where my senses couldn't recognize reality.

A voice came and went, words muttered unintelligibly. Someone said my name and I opened my eyes to a blurry world of colors and shapes. Strong hands effortlessly lifted me from the hard floor onto a soft surface, as if gravity didn't exist. At last, the angels had finally come for me.

I fell asleep again, then woke when my clothes were being tugged off, and it confused me because I didn't know angels were required to dress me. Whoever or whatever it was, I didn't fight it. I didn't have the strength.

A blanket floated over me, then another one.

I drifted back to the recesses of my mind where it was safe, where I was warm in my bed, snuggled under a fluffy comforter.

I heard my name again.

My right arm was being straightened, and a prick on my skin stung. Nobody told me there was pain in Heaven. I yelped in protest and tried to bend my arm, yet it wouldn't move.

STAND YOUR GROUND

I shook my head to clear my blurry eyesight. A hazy form came and went, and during a moment of cognizance, I reached to push it away. It was the touch of a warm hand, strong, a man's hand, yet gentle.

I thrashed and mumbled.

A bright light bounced from my left to my right, and I feebly put my hand up to shade my eyes from the blinding glare. Then glorious warmth flowed into my body, and finally I was at peace. Dying wasn't so bad after all.

"Ella, you're going to be okay."

Huh? I thought I said. I opened my eyes.

"Ella, if you can hear me, you need to try to stay awake. This is Kyle. I've given you IV fluids I had in my medic kit. It should stabilize you. As soon as I can, I'll go into town to get antibiotics for you at the hospital."

I mumbled incoherently.

"It's me, Kyle. I found you unconscious in the treehouse. You've been hurt somehow, and you have a long gash on your leg. I cleaned it and sutured it the best I could."

I willed my eyes to focus on the face inches away staring at me. The face was familiar. I recalled him now. We'd been traveling on a train. "Oh, you're Tommy's brother. I thought you were an angel."

"I've been called a lot of things," he said, laughing, "but never an angel. You're not dead yet, so stay with me."

"I wish I was dead. I was ready to die."

"No, you're going to be okay."

I turned on my side and my hand fell across the side of the bed. A wet nose nudged my fingers. "Ruger, is that you?"

"It is," Kyle confirmed. "When I heard the gunshots, Ruger ran out of the house. We weren't quite sure where you were, so on a whim, I handed Ruger one of your shirts and let him get a good sniff. I told him to find you, and he took off running. I followed him to the spring, and that's when I remembered you said you were going to take a bath."

I rubbed Ruger between the eyes and up along the flat part of his forehead. "You're a good dog."

"When we got here, Ruger started acting odd, growling, and the ruff on his back stood up. I told him to find you, and he went to the base of the treehouse then sat. He's trained well. I used the pulley to bring him up here. I was afraid he'd run off."

I took a handful of Ruger's fur and massaged along his back, working my way up to his ears. "You understand, don't you, boy?" He answered by licking my hand.

"Ella, how'd you hurt yourself?"

I sniffled, hiding my face, trying to not to cry. A welling of sorrow formed deep inside my soul, full of images I could never forget. The sounds of crunching bones. The severed arm, fingers still clutching the pistol. I let out a mournful sob of sorrow and death, and the tears flowed easily.

"Ella, what's wrong?" Kyle asked gently. "I'm here for you. You're going to be okay." He placed a hand on my arm, rubbing it.

"I want to die." I hiccupped. "I couldn't help him."

"Who couldn't you help?"

"Tommy."

"Tommy was here? That makes no sense, Ella. You're the one who needed help, and he didn't help you. He's good for nothing, but I'll set him straight once and for all. Tell me where he is."

"We have to help him. I have to get up." I pushed myself up with my good arm.

"You're not going anywhere," Kyle said, restraining me. "Stay here and I'll go look for Tommy."

"No! Don't! It's useless." My head dropped back to the pillow.

"If he left you here bleeding, he should have at least gotten help for you. I'll go find him."

I squeezed Kyle's arm hard. "He's dead."

CHAPTER 26

Kyle stood and palmed a hand over the top of his head. "What are you talking about? I saw Tommy less than an hour ago. Ella, you're hallucinating again. You were mumbling all sorts of things."

"Kyle," I coughed out, "listen to me. Tommy is dead."

"What do you mean?" Kyle gave me a pained expression.

"He was killed."

"By who?"

I shook my head, recalling my uncle's words. "Not by who, by *what*. By whatever did this to my leg." I tossed the blanket off my legs, and for the first time I saw how badly my leg was damaged. The cut was from my upper thigh to the middle of my calf, just missing the tendons of my knee. The stitches Kyle used to patch me together were bloodied, reminding me of how a Thanksgiving turkey looked with thread holding its legs together. I flexed my toes and bent my knee, testing them to make sure I still had the use of my leg.

Kyle knelt by my side. "You're telling me the same thing that nearly killed you, killed my brother?"

I nodded.

"What was it?"

"I'm not really sure. It must have been some type of wolf or a mutated one. It was huge, the size of a lion, with long fangs and claws."

STAND YOUR GROUND

I gave Kyle a condensed version of what happened, from me taking a bath, to thinking Tommy had snuck up on me and pushed me back into the water. I told him about seeing the beast for the first time, and how it was looking at me like I was prey. I told him how Tommy had stumbled upon me, and how I tried to warn him, but I was in shock and couldn't form my words right.

"Kyle, he tried to help me by distracting the beast so I could make an escape."

"Tommy did that for you?"

"He did. He gave up his life to save me."

Kyle hung his head, and kneaded his temples. After several long seconds he said, "I was ready to disown him as my brother. He's dead? Are you sure?"

"I'm sorry, Kyle. He is."

"Did he die quickly?"

"I don't think he felt any pain. It was very quick. He was no match for the thing, and he had no chance." I placed my hand on Kyle's shoulder. "He saved me, Kyle. Your brother gave up his life so I could live. You need to be very proud of him for doing that."

"Where is his body?"

"I'm not sure. The thing carried him away."

"Which direction did it go?"

"It headed south into the woods. It disappeared like it was never there."

Kyle stepped over to a table and turned on one of the lanterns. "I'll go find it and hunt it down right now," he said, retrieving his rifle he had leaned against a chair.

"Don't! It's already dark."

"I'm not going to leave my brother in the woods."

"Kyle, he's gone," I pleaded. "His soul is already with your parents. You can't risk your life for someone who is already dead, even if it's your only brother."

"I can give him a proper burial."

"There won't…be much to bury."

Kyle's mouth hung open as he tried to digest what I had said. I hated to be brutal, but unless he fully understood the situation, he'd be the next victim.

"You're right," Kyle finally admitted. "It would be foolish of me to go out into the night with my guns blazing. I'll stay here with you tonight." Kyle checked the window locks, twisted them to make sure they were locked. He closed the blinds and wedged a chair under the doorknob to reinforce the door. "I'll sit in this chair so I can stay awake. You need to try to sleep because your body needs to heal. The cut was clean, but you'll need antibiotics. I'll go into town and raid the pharmacy."

"You won't need to," I said. "My dad had a friend in pharmaceutical sales who happened to be a prepper. He used to give my dad all sorts of freebies, so we should have antibiotics at the house."

"Okay then. We'll spend the night here, and first thing in the morning, I'll get you to the house even if I have to carry you there myself."

I smiled, but without much mirth.

Kyle checked my IV and straightened out the line which had become twisted.

"What did you give me?"

"Fluids to stabilize your blood pressure. I carry my medical supplies wherever I go. Good thing too, otherwise, you might not have made it."

"Thank you for finding me."

"You should thank Ruger. He was the one who led me to you. He's a good dog, and is your dog now."

I patted the bed to invite Ruger up. He tentatively placed a paw on the edge, glanced at the bed and the covers, then effortlessly jumped without putting any pressure on me or my wounded leg. He stepped over me and spun a couple of times before pillowing into the bed. He curled into a little ball, tucked his head down, and didn't move after that. I supposed he sensed I was wounded, and in his own way, he was trying to comfort me.

During the night I slept fitfully, half afraid I wouldn't wake up, and half afraid Kyle would fall asleep, and that beast would find a way to the treehouse to finish us off.

My dreams were jagged and bounced all over the place from childhood memories to my brush with death. I sweated, shivered, cried, and tossed and turned until finally it was morning.

I woke to find Kyle had dozed off sitting in the chair. "Kyle? Wake up. It's morning."

He jerked awake. "Are you okay?"

"I will be. Let's get going."

"Let me check your leg first." He palpated my leg, and with a touch like a feather, ran his hands over it. He tenderly inspected the stitches, and lastly he placed both hands on each side of my wounded leg.

"What are you doing?" I asked.

"Trying to determine if there is an infection. Your leg would be getting hot if it was infected. Whatd'ya think I was doing?"

"I frankly didn't know."

Suddenly I became self-conscious and aware of how I must have looked. My hair was a tangled mess, my fingernails dirty, and my clothes torn and—

"Kyle, why are my clothes hanging on the table?"

"To dry."

"How did they get there?"

"I put them there, Ella. I had to remove them. You were hypothermic and shivering uncontrollably when I found you. I had to take your clothes off."

I pulled the blanket over my shoulders.

"You're embarrassed, aren't you?" Kyle said, grinning.

"No," I answered quickly. "Don't laugh, it's not funny."

"I'm not. I've seen plenty of naked women."

"Oh? You have?"

"No, wait. That came out wrong. Remember, I was a medic. I've studied anatomy so I'm aware of what the human body looks like. You needed help, and I helped you. There's no need for you to be embarrassed."

"Okay. Please don't tell anybody."

"I won't."

"Thanks."

"I need to check outside. Get dressed and then we'll go." Kyle handed me my clothes then shouldered his rifle before stepping out onto the treehouse porch. Ruger went with him. I threw my clothes on, gritting my teeth because it hurt like the devil to put my jeans on.

* * *

We left the treehouse and slogged up the hill to the house, Ruger following behind us. Kyle had to carry me part of the way when the weight on my leg became too much.

Ruger kept watch. Every few steps he'd stop and let his eyes roam over the countryside. His ears were cocked and he'd turn them, independently of each one, listening. When he decided there was no threat, he loped to catch up with us.

After what felt like a five mile hike, we reached the house. May came running out to greet us.

"Ella! I was so worried about you!" May exclaimed. "I wanted to go look for you last night but Uncle Grant wouldn't let me." Her eyes dropped to my leg and my shredded jeans. "What happened to you? You're hurt. Let me help you."

May looped her arm around my waist and we hobbled into the house. Uncle Grant met us at the door.

"Ella, I prayed all night you were okay," Uncle Grant said. "Come sit down on the sofa. I'll get you and Kyle something to eat and drink. Tommy, Kyle, and I searched for you. I heard gunshots, but couldn't determine where they came from. Was that you?"

"It was. Tommy found me."

"Where is he?" Uncle Grant asked.

I paused a long second before answering, trying to collect my thoughts about the broken windows, Uncle Grant's dog taken, and why he retreated to the cellar. The beast couldn't get him there.

"Tommy is dead," I said with a heavy heart.

"He is? What happened?" Uncle Grant glanced at Kyle, who nodded slightly to confirm my statement. "Drink this. You'll feel better." Uncle Grant handed me a cup of hot tea.

I took a few sips.

"Kyle, I'm so sorry to hear about your brother." Uncle Grant patted Kyle on the back. "I'll help you bury him. What was it, a hunting accident?"

"No," I said. "It was the same thing that was in your house, who took your dog. The same thing that made you lock yourself in the cellar killed Tommy. I was there when it happened."

Uncle Grant retrieved a blanket and put it over my shoulders, then refilled my teacup. May was sitting next to me, listening. "Why didn't you tell us?"

"I wasn't sure if what I saw was real or not," Uncle Grant said. He went to a window and looked out upon the land. "A few nights ago I had tied one on really good, feeling sorry for myself and everything. My wife leaving me and taking our only son. I passed out on the sofa."

"We figured you had been here when we found the empty bottles on the floor."

Uncle Grant shrugged noncommittally. "My dog kept barking and running around, so I figured he was barking at a coon or possum. I opened the back door," he pointed to the door near the fireplace, "to let the dog out to chase it, but he refused to go outside. I was drunker than a skunk,

STAND YOUR GROUND

and really needing to take a leak, so while I was in the bathroom, all hell broke out in the den. Glass breaking, the dog going bat-shit crazy. I grabbed the rifle I had stashed in the bathroom and went to find out what was going on. Jesus Christ Almighty, I couldn't believe what I was seeing. This thing—"

"Did it look like a wolf from the Jurassic period?" I asked.

"It did. I thought I was hallucinating." Uncle Grant paused. "I need a drink. Can someone get me one?"

"It's kind of early for a drink, Uncle Grant."

"Not now, Ella."

"I'll get it for you," Kyle said. He returned in a few moments with a shot of bourbon and handed the glass to Uncle Grant, who tossed it back in one swallow. "Thanks. I aimed my rifle at that animal and shot, but with everything going on, I didn't hit it. I tried again but my rifle jammed. I mean, how much more could go wrong? That thing crouched, preparing to jump to finish me off, but in the confines of the room it didn't have enough space to maneuver, and when it landed on the wood floor, it lost traction. I took my chances and hoofed it to the cellar and bolted myself in." Uncle Grant hung his head. "I couldn't help my dog. I feel real bad about it too."

"Don't, Uncle Grant," I said. "There was nothing you could do."

"After that, I lost track of time. I could hear it in the house, its claws tapping on the wood floors. I couldn't sleep. I was afraid if I fell asleep it would find a way into the cellar. It was driving me insane."

"You looked like a wild man when we found you," I said.

"I thought I'd lose my mind."

"Uncle Grant, what are we going to do?"

"Ella, we are going to hunt that thing down and kill it, so it can't hurt anything else."

"How?"

"I'll figure that out later. For now, we are going to bug in for a few days. Nobody, I mean *nobody,* goes anywhere by themselves. At least two people together at all times. Is that clear?"

We nodded in unison.

"We are all going to learn to be proficient with firearms, and that means you too, May. Got it? No more excuses for not learning," Uncle Grant said, looking pointedly at May.

May nodded. "I'll do my part."

Afterwards, Uncle Grant prepared breakfast for us of venison steak and fresh dewberries he had picked a few days prior and stored in the cellar where it was cool. He rounded it out with camp biscuits he prepared then placed in foil to bake in the coals from the previous night. We had all the fresh milk to drink, albeit warm. Kyle stood guard while Uncle Grant cooked the venison and camp biscuits. Since May wasn't proficient enough in handling firearms, and I was still weak, Uncle Grant instructed us to stay inside.

He said it would be best for me to rest so I could fight another day.

I did live to fight another day.

We all would, but for now, we were safe, we were together, and that was all that really mattered at that moment.

When the going got tough, we did what was necessary to survive. We successfully escaped my hometown, we fought off the attackers who had planned to execute the president, and we came together as a team.

We stood our ground.

And I'm proud to say I did too. It wouldn't be the last time I'd be required to take a stand either.

CHAPTER 27

Central Texas
Fifty Years in the Future

"Ella? Ella! Stop! Don't talk anymore." Teddy removed his glasses and pinched the bridge of his nose.

"Hmm?" I gazed at Teddy, wondering what was the matter with him.

"You're shaking."

"I am?" I clasped my wrinkled hands together to quiet their trembling. "I was back there," I said apologetically.

"You were worrying me. I don't think it's a good idea to continue." He flicked off the tape recorder. "It's too horrible for you to remember what happened to you. I can't make you do this anymore." Teddy gathered his pencils and pads, opened his satchel, and tossed them where they fell to the bottom.

"But what about your thesis?" I asked. "You can't quit now."

"Screw the thesis. I had no idea your experiences were so horrific. You're reliving everything bad that happened."

"What did you expect? An ice cream party?"

"No, but—"

"The United States was decimated. Millions of people died during the initial attack, and the survivors were left to fend for themselves."

STAND YOUR GROUND

"Don't you realize what's happening to you?" he asked.

"Like what?"

"You're trembling all over. You're incoherent at times. Your eyes rolled into your head when you were talking about Tommy being killed by that, that—"

"We called them tearawolves."

"Right, that's what you said earlier. They're so scarce there's only two in museums. What exactly was it?"

"Wolves that mutated from the biological agent."

"That happened very quickly," Teddy commented. "I've never heard of mutations like that."

"The people responsible had set up a secret lab west of here where they did animal testing to see what would happen when the animals were exposed to the biological agent used in the attack. Some of them mutated, including the wolves. The tearawolves escaped when the scientists died."

"A lab? I never heard of a lab."

"My uncle told us about a foreign country that had been quietly purchasing land west of where the ranch was located. Over several years, they bought about ten thousand acres, and my uncle also said some men had visited him, and offered to pay him and my dad double over market value for the ranch."

"What did your uncle say to them?"

"He pointed a rifle at them and told them never to come back."

Teddy laughed. "I can imagine them running away. Still, I don't quite understand something. How did you discover the lab?"

"When our supplies became low, we foraged for anything we could find. We stumbled upon the lab by accident."

"What did you find?"

I shook my head. "I don't want to get into that right now."

"Too much?"

I nodded.

"What about the tearawolves? Were there many more of them? Were others attacked?"

"Teddy, I'm trying to be truthful, and not give you some sort of sanitized version of what happened to us. I'm especially against telling you what you want to hear. Not everybody lived happily ever after. This isn't the Hallmark Channel."

"What's that?"

"Never mind. It was a joke."

"I don't think we should continue," Teddy said. "Regardless of how you look or feel, you're not a young woman anymore. I'm not insulting you, I'm stating a fact. Fifty years of surviving without modern conveniences or medicine would do a number on anyone."

I steepled my hands in front of me. "I don't think it's me you need to worry about," I replied. "The truth isn't pretty. Freedom isn't pretty. People died for the freedom you have now, so you can damn well listen to their story. You began this, so you need to finish it."

"Ella, it's late, I'm tired." Teddy slouched in his chair. "Let's do this another day."

I sat forward and put my hands on the table. With renewed conviction I said, "No. We'll do this now."

Teddy looked at me long and hard, staring right through me, challenging me. His jaw was clenched and sharp. He had some fight in him after all. I liked that.

"I have a suggestion," I offered. "Let's take a short break. Stretch our legs. Get some fresh air."

Alright," Teddy said. "That's a good idea. I could also use something to eat."

"I have banana bread I made with wheat I grew. It's not very sweet, but it's filling and will stick to your ribs."

"Sounds good." Teddy stood and stretched.

I reached into my satchel to get a piece of banana bread I had wrapped in a hand towel.

"How about I make you a fresh pot of coffee?" Teddy offered.

"I'd like that."

"Don't take the banana bread out yet," he said. "Let's eat it with a cup of coffee. Also, I have a question."

"Go on."

"History has told us the reason for the biological attack, which you guessed correctly was to steal the pod's new technology—that's a story all by itself—and the nation survived—"

"Barely," I reminded him.

"Right, and all of that is in the history textbooks being used in schools today."

"I'm glad to hear it."

"But what's not in the textbooks is what happened to everyday people like yourself."

"I survived. That's what mattered. Winning against evil mattered."

STAND YOUR GROUND

"It does. I also want to know what happened to Kyle and May."

I didn't answer immediately, letting my thoughts turn to Kyle and what happened after he saved me. I reached to my shirt, lifting out the necklace I found in the pool. I never took it off once I put it on. Perhaps it did bring luck because I could have bled to death in the treehouse, yet I didn't.

I thought about my sister May, so fragile compared to me. She wasn't though. Dynamite definitely came in small packages.

My dad was right, and I recalled his sage advice from years ago. *When you get older, when things are tough, when your mom and I are dead and buried, when your friends have their own lives, you'll understand your sister will be the only person you can count on.*

My friends did leave, my parents died, yet I still had my sister. Family was there for each other by supporting one another and helping when the going got tough. My dad taught me that with how he helped his own brother. He lived by a certain code, one which still lived in me; a code of doing whatever needed to be done to survive.

I sometimes wondered why I lived, and I now believe it was so I could tell my story, about the time immediately after the attack, unfiltered, with all the triumphs and tragedies. Not only mine, but everyone else's whose voices were silenced.

During everything that happened, I never lost hope, though, because hope was for the living. I was still hopeful, and though my life wasn't what I thought it would be, I'd lived an honest one, a meaningful one.

I had no regrets.

The End

BEHIND THE SCENES: A NOTE FROM THE AUTHOR

Hi readers, this is Chris. Well, I hope you enjoyed Book 1 of the American Strong series. I tried to do something different by mixing some sci-fi into the story, yet not straying too far away from reality. Having a secret lab could lead to all sorts of possibilities in future books!

I have a follow up book planned about the survivor's struggles, and I hope to get it out as fast as I can. If you'd like to be put on the mailing list for notification, email me at Chris.Pike123@aol.com to let me know.

The inspiration for the series came to me while driving to work one day on Interstate 10. I was traveling east, stuck in traffic, when clouds peeked over the Loop 610 and I-10 exchange. I wondered what would happen if the clouds were the result of biological warfare. A morning commute led to this book.

Deciding on character names is always a difficult task because names need to be easy to spell and remember, yet not be overused. Since this book was about two sisters, I decided to name the main female character from genealogy research I did several years ago. I discovered a gggrandmother whose name was Cindrella (not Cinderella), but since the name is too long to keep for a book, I shortened it to Ella. The character May was named after my grandmother's sister, who died as a young teenager. Even when my grandmother got into her 80s, she still talked about and missed her sister.

For those of you who have read the EMP Survivor Series, I'm still thinking about a short series with Nico and Kate after they leave the Double H Ranch. If you haven't read the series, here are the books in order.

Available books in the EMP Survivor Series:
Unexpected World – Book 1
Uncertain World – Book 2
Unknown World – Book 3
Unwanted World – Book 4
Undefeated World Book – 5

The series is available on Amazon

BEFORE YOU GO...

* * *

One last thing. Thank you, thank you, thank you for downloading this book. Without the support of readers like yourself, Indie publishing would not be possible.

I've received a lot of emails from my readers, and for those who have written me, you know I always answer your emails, and I don't spam either.

An easy way to show your support of an Indie author is to write an honest review on Amazon. It does several things: It helps other readers make a decision to download the book, and it also allows the author to understand what the readers want. For example, my readers asked for no F-bombs or adult situations. I listened and followed through with the requests. I've learned good writing and editing is extremely appreciated and I will always strive for that.

So please consider writing a review. It will be forever grateful. A few words or one sentence is all it takes.

* * *

I've had a lot of help along the way from some special people, first and foremost my husband, Alan. He was the brains behind the expert firearm and knife content in the book, and was my consultant on shootouts.

Writing a book is not a solitary undertaking, and many people have helped me. Special thanks go to those who have inspired, cheered, edited, proofed, provided cover art, formatted, legal advice, narrated, or were sounding boards: daughters Michelle and Courtney, son-in-law Cody, editor Felicia, proofer Mick, cover artist Hristo, friends Anne, Mikki, and Mary, and formatter Kody. A special thanks goes to you ladies and gents.

For my readers who have written me and have connected with me on Facebook, y'all are the best! You've encouraged me and have allowed me a glimpse into your lives. I am truly honored. Thank you. For anyone else who would like to connect with me, email me at Chris.Pike123@aol.com.

I'm on Facebook at Author Chris Pike.

So until next time, remember to read, enjoy, learn, and save some more food.

All the best,
Chris

Made in the USA
Columbia, SC
07 September 2018